NEUTRAL
———————

JANE WASHINGTON
JAYMIN EVE

Copyright 2018 © Jane Washington and Jaymin Eve. All rights reserved.
The authors have provided this book for your personal use only. It may not be re-sold or made publicly available in any way. **Copyright infringement is against the law.** Thank you for respecting the hard work of these authors.

Washington, Jane
Eve, Jaymin
Neutral

www.janewashington.com
www.jaymineve.com

Edited by David Thomas and Josephine Banks
www.josephinebanksofficial.com/editing

ISBN: 978-1729651537

For the shippers.

GLOSSARY

click – **minute**
rotation – **hour**
sun-cycle – **day**
moon-cycle – **month**
life-cycle – **year**

ONE

EMMY

Dying was easier than I expected, but being brought back to life? That was hard. Death had come in a flash of pain, blinding in its intensity. It completely overwhelmed me, and then it was over ...

Until it wasn't.

I felt Willa calling me back. Her voice was pleading with me but I was safe and comfortable in death and I didn't want to return to all that pain. In typical Willa fashion, she didn't give me a choice. She dragged me back through the darkness, healing me along the way. I could feel my body mending, becoming stronger as power tingled through me. There was chaos around me, sounds battering against my ears and heat blasting across my cheeks.

Soon, the unidentifiable sounds were merging into voices and I was slipping back into unconsciousness—although it was a living unconsciousness this time.

I drifted in this state for some time as everything settled into a buzzing darkness, and while I probably could have woken myself up and opened my eyes, a part of me wasn't ready. I liked to live my life in an orderly fashion. I liked knowing exactly what to expect from every single sun-cycle—except for Willa, of course ... she was the only disruption I accepted. There was nothing orderly about dying, and being dragged back from death was even more chaotic. I wasn't sure what I would see when I opened my eyes, or even where I would be. I half expected to have been dropped in some in-between state—a world reserved for dwellers who haven't had the pleasure of dying completely.

Eventually, I couldn't hide any longer.

My lashes fluttered, light seeping in through the edges. Pain no longer touched any part of me, and by the time my eyes were fully open, I could feel strength coursing through me. Swinging my legs over the side of the bed I had been laying on, I glanced around the room in confusion. Everything was white. I groaned, my head falling into my hands as crystal-clear memories suddenly rushed back to me. As I pondered the impossibility of what had happened, the door opened and someone walked into the room.

Or ... some*thing* walked into the room.

"You are awake, Sacred One." It was Donald's voice.

I let my head fall back into my hands but then paused, her greeting finally penetrating my reeling mind. I glanced around the room. Willa wasn't with me, so who was Donald calling a 'Sacred One?' And where the hell was my sister? I knew she was the one who had saved me, but she wasn't there anymore. I was completely alone, apart from Donald.

"Where is the Sacred One?" I finally asked.

Donald pointed at me. I moved out of the way of her finger. Her finger moved with me. I groaned again.

"You definitely malfunctioned, didn't you? Where's Willa?"

"Sacred Willa the Great and Only is sleeping," Donald answered.

If it were possible for a person to sit on a bed and blink sarcastically at a Topian server, that was what I was doing.

"Where is the Great and Only sleeping?" I asked dryly.

"In her new bedroom," Donald answered helpfully.

"Can you take me there?" I asked.

Donald shook her head. "I cannot, Sacred One."

"Why not?" I pushed to my feet, suddenly filled with exasperation. My emotions felt a little more erratic than usual.

"Sacred Willa is being guarded and is not allowed visitors," Donald informed me, sounding downright cheerful.

"Who is guarding her?" I asked, glancing down at myself.

I had only just noticed that I was wearing deep green robes, the colour almost inching toward blue. It wasn't a colour I even recognised; it seemed to morph from blue to green as I moved my arm, shifting the robe around. Weird.

"Sacred Coen the Mighty and Painful, Sacred Rome the Great and Strong, Sacred Aros the Beautiful and Sexy, Sacred Yael who is better than the others, and Sacred Siret who told me all their proper titles."

I couldn't help a snort. "Right. Can you maybe go and ask them again? Because when they said that they were guarding her, they didn't mean from *me*."

"As you wish, Sacred One." Donald made a short, snappy bow, and then she disappeared.

"Sacred One?" I asked again, just as confused as the first time ... but she was already gone.

Too agitated to sit still any longer, I started to wander around the unfamiliar room, touching random books and objects until Donald returned, popping back into existence at the entrance to the room. The sudden appearance didn't startle me like it normally would have. It was almost as though I had sensed her coming—a tiny vibration through the air, disrupting the otherwise silent and still space. I'd never been able to do *that* before.

"Where am I?" I asked her, before she could say anything else.

"You are in the bedroom, Sacred One."

"Why do you keep calling me that?"

"You are a god. A Sacred One."

I froze, almost believing it for a moment, because I *knew* that I had died, and now I was wearing robes ... but it was still impossible. I finally shook my head. Donald was malfunctioning again, that was all.

"Who's bedroom?" I asked her, waving my hand around at the space.

"This is the secret dwelling of the Sacred Neutral."

"The Sacred Asshole …" I mused, narrowing my eyes.

"The Sacred Neutral," Donald corrected me.

"The Sacred *Asshole*," I re-corrected her. "You've been saying it wrong this whole time."

She gasped, a small mechanical-sounding noise. "I'm so sorry! I will go and apologise to him immediately!"

She rushed out of the room and I followed her, through a sprawling white living room, down a short white hallway, through a tall white door and straight into a—*you guessed it*—completely white bathing room. Cyrus was standing beneath a narrow rainfall of water directed from several little spurts in the ceiling. The whole space was filling up with steam; only half a white stone wall with several glass vials and selections of soaps lined along the top blocked my view of a *very* naked Neutral God.

"*What the fuck*?" Cyrus yelled, leaning forward and planting his hands on the half-stone wall. "How many times do I have to tell you *not* to barge into the bathing room whenever you need to apologise for something, Donald?"

He flicked his eyes to me as she cowered back a

few steps, and I tried to force my eyes to stay focused on his face. I then had to force my eyes to narrow angrily.

"Don't talk to her like that." I pointed a finger at him.

"I'm so sorry, Sacred Asshole!" Donald was doing her little bow thing again.

I quickly pulled her upright. Cyrus sighed, his gaze still locked on me, apparently forgetting all about Donald.

"You're awake," he noted, his voice several degrees calmer, the tone deepening a little with some kind of message that I wasn't receiving.

I swallowed. "You should ... ah ... I'll just wait outside."

I quickly turned on my heel, his chuckle floating out after me as I dragged Donald back into the other room and slammed the door behind me.

"Where's Willa?" I demanded, as soon as we were back in the living room. "They said I could see her, didn't they?"

"Yes, Sacred One. Willa is on Sacred Pica's platform."

"Where is that?"

Donald pointed a finger ... apparently in the direction of Pica's platform. I sighed, rubbing at my temples. I was going to have to wait for Cyrus. For some reason I expected him to stay in the bathing room for a long time. To make me wait on his 'sacred' presence. He was arrogant in that way: acting as though both of the worlds revolved around him. All gods were the same ... except for the Abcurses. Their world revolved around Willa—conveniently embodying the only redeeming quality in any god I'd met to date.

"How are you feeling?"

The low voice startled me. The first thing to actually startle me since I woke up. Somewhere in the back of my mind, I must have heard him approach, but I had been too busy in my own thoughts. Turning, I found Cyrus a few feet away, wrapped in a towel. Sprinkles of water peppered right across his chest, leading down the muscled ridges of his torso to the angled lines dipping below his towel. *Holy crap*, the Sacred Asshole was ...

Average, I lied to myself.

I forced my eyes up to his face, drawing on the discipline that had gotten me through my life as a dweller. I wouldn't allow myself to cave to this bastard. Sure, we had kissed and it had shaken me to my core, but that was before. Before I died. I was a changed dweller, now. I was already in well over my head, and Cyrus was a distraction that I didn't need.

"I'm fine," I said shortly. "I want to see Willa. Take me to her."

Cyrus didn't seem to have the same aversion to looking at me as I did to looking at him. His eyes raked along my body, drinking in my features as though I were the most interesting thing to ever interrupt his bathing time.

"Nice robes," he finally commented, ignoring my demand. "I've never seen any that colour before."

I crossed my arms over my chest, feeling somewhat exposed, even though I was literally covered from throat to feet. I finally understood what Willa had been talking about though: the robes were extremely comfortable. The material was silky and light, brushing across my body. Wait ... *was I wearing underwear?*

There was no way I could have a Willa moment in front of the Asshole of Topia. I needed to assess that situation as soon as it was safe to do so.

"I'm going to give you to the count of three," I said slowly, without inflection. "Take. Me. To. Willa. If you do not take me to Willa by the time I hit three, I will—"

My words were cut off by his lips. He had moved

so fast that I didn't even see it coming—or maybe I didn't want to see it, since I was trying very hard not to look at him closely. All breath whooshed out of me as our bodies crashed together: his so strong and hard, and mine completely disloyal as it moulded against him. On instinct, I went onto my tiptoes, wrapping my arms around his neck and pulling myself closer.

The only other kiss to ever rock me was Atti's, and while I had enjoyed kissing Atti very much ... kissing Cyrus was different.

It was soul destroying.

A part of me would always mourn Atti. He was my perfect match in so many ways. We had been comfortable. We had fit together. I tried to remember that comfortable, familiar feeling as Cyrus kissed me into oblivion, but it was slipping away from me faster that I could grasp it.

"I'm so fucking angry at you," he murmured against my lips.

I pulled back, shaking my head as I planted a hand against his chest, as though that would keep him from kissing me again.

"You're mad at me? I'm so shocked. What did I do this time?" My sarcastic drawl had his forehead creasing, his eyes turning even stormier.

He jerked me a little harder against him, and my body ached—in the best kind of way. "You put yourself in a position to be used by Staviti. To be hurt. To be killed. You brought attention to yourself. You made the gods aware of you."

I growled then, struggling to free myself. "I did none of those things. I have always been the perfect dweller. The Abcurses brought Willa into this world, and where she goes, I go. So this is all on the gods. This is *their* fault!"

I placed both of my hands on his chest now and shoved with all of my might. "Now take me to my sister or I will make your eternal life a living hell."

He made a noise that had every hair on my arms standing on end. Cyrus could be scary when he Neutraled out. He stepped away from me and as he spun to head toward his bedroom, it sounded like he said *you already are*. But I must have misheard him. I wasn't *in* his life enough to make it a living hell. Well, except for being a dead person in his bed for a little while and walking in on his bathing time.

When he was gone, I realised that Donald was still in the room. She was standing in the corner, staring at the floor. I'd completely forgotten about her as Cyrus stole all of my attention. He had a way of doing that. As I stepped closer to her, I pushed down the small pang in my chest. The practical side of me knew that this was no longer Willa's mum ... or my adoptive mother, but it was hard to believe that when she was just standing there with her wild blond hair and vacant expression. She looked just the same as she always had. She'd been a mess of a dweller in real life, and now she was a mess of a server. Willa had told me about the cart transporting dweller bodies past the seventh ring, where they were made into Topian servers. She had also mentioned hearing something about there being requirements to become a server. It would make sense, seeing how Donald acted now. If the dwellers had boasted undesirable characteristics in their previous life, they were probably disqualified from becoming servers. It didn't surprise me that Staviti had forgotten all about Donald after creating her and sending her back to Willa. She had been a message, a threat.

Don't mess with me.

She was never supposed to be an actual server.

"Donald, why did you say that I'm a god?" I asked her gently.

I had no idea why I bothered. She was definitely malfunctioning again, and yet ... I couldn't just let it go. She had suggested it; I needed to know why. Even when she malfunctioned, there was still a reason behind the things she did and said.

"You are a god now, Sacred One. Sacred Willa used her sacred gifts, and now you are a Sacred One."

"It's ... that isn't possible," I argued, even though a tiny spark in the back of my mind spluttered with hope. I *wanted* to believe her. "Dwellers don't become gods. This is a fact. I know my facts, Donald. I can tell you all about facts."

Cyrus's low chuckle had me spinning around. A relieved sigh left me when I found him fully dressed in his signature white robes. "You do have a remarkable grasp on a seemingly endless supply of mostly useless dweller facts, Emmanuelle ... but in this instance, Donald is correct. You are a god now. And dwellers *do* become gods. Your sister is one of them, or have you forgotten already?"

I let out a growl. "You better be kidding me. I refuse to be a god. I am not one of you evil, selfish bastards."

Cyrus strode closer and it took everything inside of me not to back away from him. Whenever he got too close, my brain fried, and I needed to stay in control.

"You're a god, bug. I didn't dress you in those

robes. They formed around your body as you healed. You were brought back from death and transformed into something else, but I don't know what you were transformed into because these robes are unlike any colour I've ever seen."

"What?" I gasped out, combing through everything he had just said for any hidden clues or evidence that we might have missed.

I wanted to believe him and I didn't want to believe him in equal measures. I had been happy as a dweller, happy to fight for a better place in the world *as* a dweller ... but I couldn't deny that something fundamental had changed inside me. Something was drastically different. If Donald and Neutral were right, and I was a god ...

What sort of god was I?

TWO

CYRUS

I wasn't going to stand around and argue about whether she was a god or not. Not when I knew that I was right.

"I'll prove it," I told Emmy, holding up a finger.

She looked at my finger as though she was trying to figure out how to forcibly detach it. I turned and strode out of the room, not waiting for a response. My weapons closet was tucked behind a false door, hidden within a crevice of the cave. It was there that I went, as Emmy waited in the other room. I knew that the only reason she hadn't stalked after me was because she was too angry or confused to move.

For some reason, I enjoyed her heightened emotions, the way she stiffened up—right from the feet to the neck. It made me want to pick her up and shock the movement back into her body, to heat her blood and press her in places just to see her give in to the pressure of my touch ... but that wouldn't help to prove my point.

I grabbed what I needed and then strode back to her, watching as she turned on her heel, whipping about to face me. I pulled the crossbow up, balanced it, and took aim.

"Wait!" she screamed, holding both of her hands up, her eyes wide and terrified. I took a step closer. She took several shaky steps backwards. "Wait ..." she repeated, as though attempting to calm a crazed person. "Cyrus ... I don't think it will work. Please don't do this. I believe you, whatever you say, just don't shoot me with that thing to prove your point. I swear, I believe you!"

I frowned, glancing down at the crossbow. "Did I pick the wrong weapon? I figured this would be preferable. More comfortable, for a dweller." I wasn't *actually* going to shoot her, but she didn't need to know that.

For a fraction of a click, the snarl started to tip up the side of her mouth again, but she quickly managed to get herself back under control. Gods, she was cute.

"It isn't the nicest way to die," she reminded me.

I set the crossbow aside. "Yes, I suppose that makes sense."

She relaxed then, the tension draining out of her shoulders, the anger flooding back into her face. I raised my right hand, directing my energy toward her.

"I will do it this way instead," I conceded.

She started forward, as though to rush me, but had barely taken two steps before I willed her to faint. Her eyes rolled back and she collapsed, but I quickly caught her, pulling her up into my arms and carrying her over to the couch. I set her down, and then crouched beside her, waiting for her to wake up and be a little less argumentative about her new, godly state. I hadn't *actually* killed her to prove my point, but she wouldn't know the difference between fainting and dying at this stage—for a god in Topia, it was all more or less the same if they were mortally wounded. Unless one of Death's weapons had been used, of course. I could hear Donald approaching behind me, her shuffle distinctive.

"This is what happens to people who barge in on me while I'm in the shower," I announced, allowing my voice to carry.

The expected gasp met my statement—but it wasn't one of abject horror, or fear. It had been a sound of ... disbelief. Excitement, even. My brow furrowed, and I turned away from Emmy, who had already begun to stir. Donald had dropped the folded towels that she had been holding, her wide eyes fixed on me, filled with wonder and gratitude. For a moment, I glanced at the folded towels now spilled over the ground. I had sent my own server away, safely out of reach of Staviti, but that meant that Donald had taken over her duties.

"What?" I asked her. I wasn't usually confused, and it irritated me to be unsure of the meaning of her reaction.

"You would make me a Sacred One?" she breathed out in reverence. "Thank you, Sacred Asshole. *Thank you.* I will do exactly as you have asked."

She bowed, her waxy face caught in what threatened to be a permanent expression of ecstatic wonder. I watched her gather the towels and walk away, too shocked to take the time needed to clear up the misconception. I turned back to Emmy instead, slipping my hand beneath her head to prop her up a little. Her hair slid silkily over my wrist, and I was momentarily distracted by the way a curl tried to wrap around my arm. She murmured something and I leaned in closer to hear her, my attention riveted to her lips, trying to make out the word that she was forming.

K ... i ... l ... l.

"Kill," she rasped, her eyes slowly opening, her pupils expanding as she locked onto me. "I am going to *kill* you!"

I held up my finger again. She grabbed it. I grabbed her wrist with my other hand. She thrust her palm into my nose, breaking it almost instantly. I reeled back, propping myself up on the floor, holding my robe to my nose to stem the blood. It was healing already, but that didn't change the fact that she had done it. And it had *hurt*. Sort of. Well, it *would* have hurt if my power hadn't naturally risen to absorb the pain—a protective reflex I had developed. She seemed to be almost as surprised as I was, pulling her hand up in front of her face and staring at it incredulously.

"I'm a god," she muttered in disbelief.

"That's what I was trying to say." I dropped the section of robe I had been holding to my nose, glancing down at the small patch of blood. *Great*, now I would have to change. "The only question is, *what* are you a god *of*?"

"That's not the only gods-damned question!" she protested, jumping to her feet. I waved my hand casually, forcing her legs to buckle so that she fell back down to the couch again. She growled out a sound, but didn't try to stand again. "That's not the only question," she repeated, narrowing her eyes on me. "How is it possible for Willa to do this? How did this happen?"

I slowly rose until I was standing before her, taking the two steps needed to box her legs in against the couch.

"How Willa managed it isn't anywhere near as important a question as how Staviti is going to react when he realises what has happened—if he doesn't already know. We need to figure out what your power is before that happens, so that you're not left completely defenceless."

"I didn't bring myself back from the dead. Shouldn't we be making a plan to protect Willa?"

"You are the evidence," I explained, leaning over a little—since she was too preoccupied with our dilemma to remember that she didn't want to be anywhere near me. "Staviti's war against Willa has already begun. Abil and Adeline, Pica, and myself—we have all joined the fight. Staviti didn't retreat because he was beaten. He retreated because he's intelligent, because he realised that Willa has an army at her back, and if he's going to defeat her, he will need an army of his own."

"What does that have to do with me?" Her voice had softened, confusion riding her tone. I inched closer. She didn't seem to mind, so I planted my hand against the couch beside her head.

"If Willa can show people that she can do this—this thing that only Staviti should be able to do—there's a chance that the other gods will choose her side."

This seemed to stun her for a moment. It was noticeable, because she always kept up with our conversations, and I never had to explain things to her over and over. Like most dwellers.

"I've been thinking," I continued. "You becoming a god might have been because of Willa's power, but your own inner strength would have had a hand in the process. The process is not an easy one to survive. You are special, for a dweller, so ... you should be proud, Emmanuelle. You are immensely strong. Again, for a dweller."

Her stunned expression tipped back into annoyance at my failed attempt to compliment her. "Why thank you, Sacred Asshole."

A trickle of amusement washed through me. I should have known Donald's new name for me didn't come from the server herself. "You're welcome."

She attempted to shove me back—and while her push was stronger than it used to be, it was still no match for my strength. I wasn't a god who used my muscle without reason, however, so I stepped back to give her the room she desired.

"You're so arrogant," she bit out, jumping to her feet. "If I annoy you that much, why the hell are you always around? Every time I turn the corner, there you are."

"I –"

I had no fucking idea how to answer that. I didn't consciously search her out, that was for sure, and yet ... she was right. I followed her around like some kind of besotted pet, insulting her at every chance and kissing her whenever she let her walls down enough for me to push through to her.

I had no idea what I was doing.

"Are you ready for me to take you to Willa?" I deflected. She lifted one eyebrow at me, but she didn't comment on my obvious discomfort with the subject.

"Yes, I need to see my sister."

"Give me a click to change," I said shortly, my

temper rearing its head again for some unknown reason.

Before she could say another word, I strode from the room. By the time I'd changed into another set of robes—dissolving my blood-stained ones with a flick of my wrist—I had myself under control again. For sun-cycles, I'd been walking on the edge of losing it. From the moment I'd found myself standing before Staviti on top of Champions Peak, something had snapped inside me. I had been too slow to stop him killing Emmy, and that realisation managed to spin me completely out of control. I couldn't even remember much of what happened during the fight. A white haze had flashed over my vision, pushing my need to deal justice to the forefront of my awareness. I had been compelled to reverse the death that Staviti had caused. Normally, my power would be unconcerned with the death of a dweller, but I was no longer the emotionless man that I had once been. Emmy had become as important—in my mind—as the Creator. Something crucial to the worlds had been snuffed out, and my energy rose in response, completely overpowering my normal control.

I couldn't figure out if my emotions were driving the shift in Emmy's importance, or if she really *was* important to Topia somehow. Was it possible for Willa to shift the balance so drastically? To make the people important to *her* also important to Topia?

"Let's go," I said, striding back into the living room and pushing the thoughts from my head.

She jumped, spinning around with wide eyes. "For Topia's sake, Cyrus, could you wear a bell or something?"

"A bell ..." I repeated. The dweller inside of her definitely made an appearance at times. "Gods do not wear bells like domesticated beasts. If we don't want you to know we're coming, you won't know it. Be grateful I gave you notice at all."

"Notice of what?" she asked, crinkling her brow.

"This," I said, reaching out and attaching myself to her arm. In a flash of energy, we were pulled from my home to a nearby platform. The air was clear and crisp, the sky bright with light and energy. I felt it fill the centre of my power, which was drawn from this world.

When I released Emmy, she leaned forward, huffing and puffing with her hands resting on her knees. "Asshole," she wheezed out.

"You need a new word," I told her dryly.

She spluttered at me for a moment, before sucking in a deep breath and straightening. "Willa's here? This is Pica's platform?"

Her composure appeared to have returned, her tone even. I took a click to look around Pica's platform.

"She's in there." I pointed toward the smaller of the marble structures. "Being cared for by Abil's sons and a crazy goddess."

"I heard that, Snow-flake."

I shuddered as the sickly-sweet voice of Pica washed over me. Fear wasn't an emotion I felt often, but Pica definitely sent unease through me. I was hit with a blast of her energy when she appeared from behind a fluffy, cloud-shaped magenta bush. Her plants didn't come from the God of Nature, that was for sure. There was nothing natural about Pica and her obsessions. Most of her plants were made to be fluffy, in varying shades of bright, too-intense colours.

"Who do we have here?" she asked, looking beyond me. She stepped closer, her robes dragging across the ground. This sun-cycle, the hem was edged in lace. The next sun-cycle, it would probably be edged in knives.

For some reason, I stepped in front of Emmy, hiding her from the sight of the Goddess of Love. "No one you need to concern yourself with," I snapped, drawing Pica's attention back to me. "We need to speak with Willa."

What the hell was I doing? We needed the other gods and goddesses to see Emmy, to realise the power that Willa had, to see the proof of it. I tried to calm the protective surge that ran through me. Unsuccessfully. Pica clapped her hands together before she spun around in a circle, her arms windmilling back and forth in some sort of dance.

"Willy, my favourite daughter!" Her voice was all dreamy.

I felt Emmy stir behind me and I hoped that for once she would keep her mouth shut. Most of the gods didn't appreciate a mouthy dweller.

Except me, apparently, I thought sarcastically.

"She's not your daughter, Pica," I reminded her. "You don't own her. Remember that keeping her here is permitted because you're keeping her safe, *not* because she belongs here. She is not a prisoner."

This was a reminder I had been forced to repeat almost every sun-cycle since our stand-off on Champion's Peak.

Pica stopped twirling, and when her eyes met mine, they were tinged with ruby tones. "I do not keep prisoners, Cyrus." Her voice grew deep, and while my first instinct was to smack her into the platform because she was seriously pissing me off, I managed to restrain myself. "I love everything I have," she continued. "I love it more than my own life. This is their sanctuary."

Love and obsession. Pica had blurred the lines between the two to the point that she couldn't even keep it straight any more.

"We need to see Willa," I reminded her.

A bright smile tilted up her cheeks. "Right! Follow me."

As we walked, I continued to manoeuvre myself between Pica and Emmy, trying to block her completely from view. Her damn robes were too bright though, they drew attention, the blues and greens shifting as she walked, almost like the colour couldn't decide what colour to be. All the gods had one solid shade, that was how it was. Except for the creator, of course. He had two colours.

Emmy's robes were going to cause a stir, and the last thing I needed was for Staviti to catch wind of her reappearance after he had killed her. Or for Pica to want to add her to her 'sanctuary'.

"I'll just pop in and see if she's awake first," Pica told us, pausing outside the room Willa had been taken to.

I'd checked on her a few times because I knew

Emmy would want to know, when she eventually woke. And ... because Willa had grown on me. She was like a walking hurricane, but somehow I enjoyed watching her cause chaos wherever she went. Of course, Willa came with a set of five asshole gods that I had to deal with, so Emmy was my preferable dweller companion. If I had to have one.

"Has she woken at all yet?" I asked.

She'd been unconscious the last time I saw her as well, asleep in the bed with all of Abil's sons. They hadn't left her side for a moment. I admired their loyalty, even while I couldn't really imagine ever feeling like that about anyone. Pica didn't answer me; she just disappeared. My hands itched to force her back with my energy, but then I'd have to deal with her insanity, and I really wasn't in the mood.

I felt a tap on my shoulder and turned to Emmy. "What?" I snapped, my emotions escaping me again.

She paused, examining me. "Have you been drinking again? You're acting very ... volatile. You need to be careful, you'll get addicted."

I closed my eyes for a beat, trying to regain my control. "No, I haven't been drinking," I bit out. "Gods cannot become addicted to drugs or alcohol. We can stop any time we want. I've been completely sober since I've been back in Topia, now that I don't have to supervise the insect farm that was Champion's Peak anymore."

Staviti had punished me by placing me on Champions Peak. He'd done it because somehow, he knew that I had helped turn Willa into whatever she was now. It had also been a power-play, of sorts. He had wanted to remind me that even though I didn't *have* to obey him, he was still the most powerful god in existence. Topia had created me a long time ago—a full-grown being born into white light. Initially, I had been a simple force: a judge, a mouthpiece for what was right and wrong, my only purpose to keep the balance in Topia. Staviti couldn't have wiped me from creation, though I had a feeling he had wanted to, and had probably even tried. Instead, he had been forced to allow me to exist. So, I existed, and as I did, I grew. I learned. I watched the dwellers and the sols and gained an understanding of their mortal emotions. I judged the gods and became acquainted with the many variants of magic and how the energies of Topia formed into powers. I watched as those powers twisted the personalities of their hosts. Love into obsession, Trickery into deviance, Creation into madness. And eventually ... I became one of them. My power twisted me into a cold judge of character. An immortal being disgusted by imperfection.

It wasn't until Willa fought her way into my life that something began to change. Her imperfection set off some kind of chain-reaction inside me—a trigger mechanism that tripped my mental processes and began a transformation in my personality. The only logical conclusion was that she was linked to Topia.

The balance had been unsettled, but instead of righting it ... Topia was righting *me* to suit ... well, *Willa-Fucking-Knight,* apparently.

Staviti was going to figure out what I had figured out eventually. Maybe he already had. The drinking had helped me get through multiple situations, but I couldn't indulge anymore. Things had escalated more quickly than I could have ever anticipated. I also didn't want to dull the sensation of being around Emmy anymore. It had helped, initially, but I was quickly switching from one addiction to another. Namely, the faint scent of vanilla that lingered on her skin. Her presence was both irritating, and somehow ... interesting.

"Why did you take the position at the Peak?" Emmy asked, breaking up our long silence. "You don't strike me as the sort of god who usually follows orders," she noted, in her far too observant way.

"I almost didn't." I stared pensively out across the land of Topia. "No god can control me, because I was not born of Staviti. Until you and Willa, I was the only being here who wasn't created from Staviti, in one way or another. I was created from the world itself, like the panteras."

"So why didn't you just refuse to go to the Peak?" she pushed.

At the time, I hadn't been able to refuse. The urge within me was too strong.

"A need," I admitted. "I was drawn there, to an important event. I didn't know what, at the time, but it was to prevent Staviti from destroying everyone on Champion's Peak. He initiated that program under false pretences, convincing the gods that it was in the best interests of both the sols, and the gods. He lied. He was trying to single out the strongest sol in each energy group. He wanted to shave off the fat—to keep them weak."

"Why would he want that?"

"I can only assume it was a grapple for power, but I'm not sure how."

"You saved them," she muttered thoughtfully.

"That was restoring the balance? Saving all those sols and dwellers?"

"I would have saved them eventually, when the time came to act. But it was Willa who forced his hand. He wouldn't have acted for another life-cycle if he hadn't found out about her."

"You still fought him," she countered. "You, Pica, Adeline, and Abil … you all made him feel outnumbered. Now he has been exposed, and all those people are still alive."

"For now," I agreed. "But the final battle is yet to come, and this one won't be between Staviti and the sols. It will be a battle of the gods—and *that* is a battle to change the worlds, Emmanuelle."

THREE

EMMY

Willa was laying on a bed surrounded by the Abcurse brothers. She was unconscious, her cheeks ashen, her breathing shallow. The Abcurses were all awake, looking as though they hadn't slept in a long time. She didn't look 'fine'—despite everyone telling me that she was. I edged toward her, but Pica slapped her hands down onto my shoulders, pulling me back.

"Oh, you *must* let the little Beta rest!" she exclaimed, shaking me just a little. "She's been through so much to get here, and she has so much healing to do. I'm sure you understand, having gone through the transition yourself only recently."

Pica released me enough to hold me out at arm's

length, her bright eyes sweeping down my front, lingering on the strange, shifting colours of my robe.

"But Willa already—" I started, turning back to look at my sister's body, before Coen caught my attention.

He was shaking his head. I glanced at the others: they all wore the same expression.

Don't bother arguing.

Apparently, Pica was a little unhinged.

"But I'm fine," I said instead, holding out my arms, before pointing back at Willa. "Why isn't she fine?"

"My little Willy is special." Pica drew back suddenly, almost in a scurry.

I blinked as Cyrus stepped around her, releasing the back of her robes—after clearly having yanked her away from me.

"Sorry," he exclaimed, sounding about as repentant as a person who had just gotten exactly what he wanted. "You were about to step on a bug." He positioned himself in front of me as Pica tried to regain her balance.

"A bug?" She jumped back another step, looking horrified, her eyes riveted to the ground.

"A very precious, very pretty, very *lovely* bug,"

Cyrus confirmed. "I think it had a tear in its little bug eye."

"Oh no!" Pica dropped to the ground, her palms flattening, her eyes still searching. She looked absolutely distraught.

"Oh yes," Cyrus returned gravely, before glancing over his shoulder at me. He lowered his voice to almost a whisper, so that I had to lean in closer to hear him. "Can we leave now?"

I frowned, shaking my head. Pica didn't scare me.

"Willa will be okay," a voice spoke from the bed, forcing us all to turn that way. Pica straightened again. Yael had been the one to speak, his words ringing with the persuasive tenor of his gift, making me want to believe him before I'd even managed to decide anything for myself.

"How do you know?" I asked, swallowing past the sudden lump in my throat.

"We can feel her," Yael replied, glancing down at Willa—he was to her left, with Siret on her right. His hand was resting across her lap, fingers possessively gripping her waist. Her head was resting against Siret's shoulder, her body half-propped against his chest.

"This is my fault," I whispered, watching the shallow breaths catch in the rise and fall of her chest. "She turned me into ..." I held my arms out, displaying the robes ... "This. And look at what it did to her."

"She's special." Pica almost sang the words, her tone holding so much joy. "Rau, my love, made her this way. He would have been so proud of her. Of our girl. She's so special. She's our little creation!"

I blinked several times, trying to comprehend what the crazy god-lady was saying. Coen was shaking his head again, and they were all wearing that same expression again.

Don't fight it.

"Is she safe here?" I asked, directing the question toward the Abcurses.

They all nodded, but Aros was the one to answer, his expression solemn.

"This is the safest place for her right now. Staviti may have declared war on Willa, but he wouldn't dare declare war on Pica."

"He is in love with me," Pica confirmed. "He always will be. To him, I am the meaning of love. His first dream and his dying wish. He cannot deny me this: my very own, special little Willy."

I was going to gag. I think one of the Abcurse brothers *had* gagged. I shook my head, but managed to bite my lip to smother any sort of reply.

"We will be back to visit the next sun-cycle," Cyrus announced, probably as creeped out by Pica as I was. His words had been delivered with some kind of warning. A warning that Pica only brushed away with a laugh and the flick of her hand.

"Willy will still be here the next sun-cycle," she assured him. "I don't plan to move her or let her go any time soon. I may never let her go!" She laughed at that.

The Abcurses seemed very grim. Cyrus's expression turned unreadable.

I felt shock, and maybe a good dose of dread, but there was a part of me that wasn't even surprised. This was just Willa's luck. If anyone could end up being protected by a psychotic goddess of 'smothering', it would be Willa.

Cyrus's fingers were suddenly wrapping around my wrist and he was drawing me out of the room, and then out of the house. He didn't pause once. I was actually running to keep up with him by the time our feet were on the marble platform again. He turned as soon as we were outside, pulling my arm up beside his head and hooking his other arm around my back.

"What are you—" I started, but the sudden shock

of my body pressed flush to his had my words meeting a quick death.

"We're going back to my home," he explained, the arm around my back tightening, drawing me up higher.

I was standing on his shoes suddenly, just to keep my feet connected to something. He stared at me for a click, his attention switching to my lips.

"Don't you dare," I warned him.

His eyes flashed back up to mine. "What?"

"Don't you dare kiss me again."

"Why the fuck not?" he growled.

"Because I think you're a ... terrible ... person! And a drunk! It doesn't matter that you're sober now, you're just a sober drunk!"

His lips twitched, almost curving into a smile. "And you're just a bug, but I seem to recall you kissing me."

"I'm allowed to. You're not."

He scowled, turning on the spot and pulling us both through a quick flash of darkness and then back into his home. He released me then and walked over to the couch, falling into the cushions, his arms crossed behind his head.

"Kiss me then," he demanded, his eyes burning even lighter and brighter than usual.

My mouth dropped open and my hands were already itching to move to my hips, to adopt a stance suitable for lecturing.

"I'll make you a deal," I found myself saying instead, my eyes narrowing as I took a step toward him.

He remained unmoving, but it almost looked like I'd shocked him a little, by *not* launching into an outraged debate.

"I don't make deals with dwellers," he finally returned, his voice low.

"I'm not a dweller anymore," I countered, reaching his legs. I climbed up onto his lap, my knees slipping to either side of his hips, my chest pressing to his, my face suddenly only an inch away from his. "I'm a god now, Cyrus. I'm your equal."

He had no response, though his hands dropped from behind his head, his fingers pressing my robe into my legs, drawing it up as his hands travelled to my hips. I had a flash of recall that I might still be without underwear, but this negotiation was too important to worry about that minor detail.

"A deal," I reminded him.

He made a sound—half a groan—and his head fell back against the couch, his eyes closing. "What are you doing to me?"

"My deal is this," I whispered, inching a little closer to his mouth. "If you help me find out what my power is and keep me safe from Staviti, I'll kiss you."

"More," he demanded, his eyes flashing open. "If I'm going to help you, you need to offer me more."

"Two kisses."

"Fucking more, bug."

I scowled, pulling back a little, but his right hand flashed up, his fingers suddenly cupping the back of my skull, and he dipped forward to win back the distance I had tried to put between us.

"Give me everything." His voice was hard, uncompromising. "If you give me everything, I'll do whatever you need. It's all or nothing, on both sides. That's what I want. That's what I'm offering. Take it or leave it."

He surged up, suddenly, taking me with him before setting me firmly onto my feet. And then he walked away, just like that.

"Let me know your decision!" he called out, a micro-click before his bedroom door slammed shut.

Asshole!

But damned if I didn't feel primed and ready to run right after him into that bedroom, which was pretty much the perfect place for Cyrus to execute his plan for 'everything'. I couldn't understand why my body was so disloyal when my mind pretty much hated everything about him.

His offer, though ... it was intriguing.

Logic was my fallback in any and all situations. One of my favourite pastimes comprised of mulling over and analysing the details of any given situation until I understood every single facet, until I understood enough to make decisions comfortably within that situation. This particular circumstance was going to be a little harder to logic out, because I really didn't know enough of the facts. Cyrus was too much of an unknown element.

If I were to be honest with myself—and I often tried to be—giving *everything* to Cyrus didn't really feel like as big a hardship as I would have expected.

The other unknown was why he had made the offer in the first place. He thought I was a bug ... and yet, I could tell that I fascinated him. Was it because I defied him at times? Could it be as simple as that? Cyrus was a god used to answering to no one, a god who was never denied. I'd seen his face the sun-cycle I quit my job as his 'dweller assistant' on the Peak, and there had been genuine shock written all over him.

Or was it simply that I was an easy and

convenient bed-mate for this moon-cycle, based on pure locality?

I doubted I'd ever truly understand Cyrus's logic, so it was better just to go with my own. Was it in mine and Willa's best interests to keep him close and as an ally? And was I willing to use my body to do that?

"I can hear you over-thinking this." Cyrus's voice was loud, even though he was still on the other side of his closed door. "This is not a decision you can make with your head, Emmanuelle. Just go with your instincts."

I snorted, my feet already moving in the direction of his room. I'd never liked arguing with people when I couldn't see them.

"Firstly," I snarled, slamming his door open, "logic can be used in every situation, except when it comes to Willa. Because she defies all natural order …"

I trailed off as I finally focused on him. My jaw dropped for a brief click before I got my facial muscles back under control. Cyrus's room was destroyed, his bed in pieces, strewn across the room, robes and sheets now nothing more than scraps of material fluttering about.

"What happened?" I asked breathlessly.

NEUTRAL

Cyrus's neutral expression—the one that I was coming to recognise as a mask he wore—slipped minutely. For a click, there was a rage so potent in his face that I sank back against the door, preparing to sprint if needed.

Just like me, though, he was very good at regaining control.

"Staviti killed you," he said simply. "When I first got you back here, I wasn't sure that you'd survive. The transition is ... difficult."

"And that bothered you?" I prompted.

I was desperate to understand him. To unravel this god who was more mysterious than any other I'd met.

"You were assigned to me," he replied moodily. "On Champions Peak. My dweller. My bug. I don't like anyone touching my possessions."

I cleared my throat. "You truly have a way with words, Cyrus. I mean, that was poetic. Truly poetic. You should title it 'mine mine mine.'"

Despite the usual arrogance I'd come to expect from the gods, his actions were unexpected. His rage, *over me,* had him destroying his room, and as he'd just said, he didn't like anyone touching his things. A bug was more important than his bedroom.

Score one for the bugs.

"Why are you in here? Did you make a decision?" he asked, moving closer to me, debris brushing the bottom of his robes as he walked through the mess.

I opened my mouth to answer, but … there were no words. I hadn't had a chance to finish my analysis, and for the first time in my life I couldn't make a decision. I couldn't figure out the best thing to do.

"Give me the full proposition," I finally choked out. "Everything. Don't leave anything out. I want the fine print."

He groaned, his eyes shifting to a stormy colour. "I don't know what it is about you, but when you get all bossy …"

Holy gods. My mind went blank as my body burned, and then a strange energy started to swirl within me. I'd never felt anything like it before, as though my insides were filled with a million burning little sparks. I closed the distance in two steps and before I could register what was happening, we were kissing like two beings who were drowning. Desperate. Consumed.

In so many ways of the worlds, I was innocent, because I chose to follow a very straight, pre-planned path. There was a 'right' way to do things, and that was always the choice I made. But in that moment, I didn't care. My path had pretty much been destroyed anyway, considering I somehow turned from a dweller into a god. An impossible feat, logically speaking. So maybe logic wasn't everything it was cracked up to be.

What the hell had happened to me? This was all Cyrus's fault, that damn assh—

A throat cleared from behind us. The mechanical sound grating and familiar. Cyrus's chest swelled beneath mine, and the heat he threw off grew to almost scorching levels.

"Donald, you're about to be decommissioned if you don't stop interrupting me," he thundered, and my body erupted in goosebumps from the power he was throwing off.

I struggled to get out of Cyrus's arms, but he didn't let me go, instead choosing to walk forward toward the poor server while still holding me, my feet a few inches off the ground.

"A thousand apologies, Sacred Asshole."

I turned my head, looking over my shoulder to find Donald bowing her head and continuing to apologise over and over. I tried not to chuckle as she repeated the words sacred and asshole twenty times in a row. It was curious that Cyrus hadn't asked her to change it yet.

"Donald!" I quickly said, drawing the server's attention. "What did you come in here for?"

She blinked a few times, before straightening from the almost-permanent bow she'd been in. "Sacred Willa is asking for you Sacred Emmy; she is awake now."

My insides went crazy, and I struggled against Cyrus. "Let me down. Now."

He tightened his grip. "What will you give me?"

I blinked at him, tilting my head further back so I could see his expression. "Are you already negotiating with me?" I asked. "Seriously?"

The right side of his mouth tilted up minutely, but it was enough that I knew he was amused. "I already told you what I want ... but I'm willing to work my way up to *everything*. For now, tell me what you'll do to go to Willa."

I swung my elbow around, clipping him across the side of the jaw. His head jerked back, but not in a way like I'd hurt him ... more in surprise.

"Did you just hit me?" he asked, before a chuckle escaped from him. "Why are you so violent, Emmanuelle?"

I snorted, crossing my arms over my chest. It was

difficult to do with him still holding me. "Says the god who threw a sol off a cliff for crying."

His gaze was dead serious when our eyes met. "We match," he told me, the words strong and sure. "Which is why I will settle for nothing less than your all. I will not take what you gave to your last dweller. Or any other. I want everything."

I swallowed roughly, trying to find the moisture that had just fled my mouth.

"Don't talk about him," I finally choked out, fighting past the heavy emotions sweeping through me.

Atti was feeling more and more like a shadow of my past, his memory shoved aside by the imposing presence of the Neutral God who was still holding me firmly against himself, refusing to let me down. That made me angry, but I needed a little more time to figure out why.

"Oh?" Cyrus goaded me, shifting me up a little higher. "So, you loved him, then. And where is he? Why wasn't he fighting for you on the mountain?"

"He's dead," I said flatly. "He did fight for me. Me and the other insects. Do you still think we match, Sacred Asshole?"

His eyes narrowed dangerously, his grip tightening on me. He had an arm banded behind my back, holding me firmly. His other hand slid up to my neck, his thumb brushing along the line from the top of my spine to the base of my skull. I reacted immediately, shivering against him, pressing closer, my anger melting into something hotter.

"Yes," he said seriously, his light eyes drinking in my reaction with an intensity that had my mind going blank again. "I really do. But I think that's enough for this sun-cycle, you've given me what I want, *for now*. I will take you to see Willa."

He set me down, and I turned immediately, striding toward Donald. I was hoping that *she* could somehow take me to Willa, because I wasn't sure that I could be trusted in Cyrus's arms again—but he only chuckled, catching my arm and drawing me back. As I spun into his chest, he drew the darkness around us and the rug disappeared from beneath my feet, hard marble taking its place. We were back on Pica's platform. I started running toward the house before Cyrus could stop me, though his footsteps—and the hurried shuffling of Donald—weren't far behind.

When I made it to the room, Willa's face was wet with tears, and when she saw me, she sobbed out my name, curling in upon herself. I rushed over to her, ignoring the others as I threw myself onto the bed and gathered her into my arms. It took me a moment to figure out what had her so distraught: she couldn't believe that I was there.

"I am alive," I reassured her over and over.

Because of her.

I held onto her tightly until I felt the Abcurses growing anxious, and then I eased back. She wasn't just mine anymore—she had her own family now. I thought back to Cyrus's words as I watched Willa with her Abcurses. He had asked for all of me, in return for all of him. Everything he had to offer: his protection included. That was what Willa had. She had each of the Abcurses in their entirety—I was sure that they would all die for her, just as she would die for them. It was *like* a family, but different. I wouldn't even hesitate to throw my life on the line for Willa, as she would for me, but I didn't have all of her, and she didn't have all of me.

I had never given myself fully to another person. Atti had been an ally, a partner. I thought that I had given him my heart, but in truth, I had only given him my love. The two were different. I had Willa's love, but the Abcurses had her *heart*.

Nobody had ever had my heart, and I wasn't sure I was ready to give it to anybody.

I wasn't sure that I even wanted everything that

Cyrus had to offer. I definitely wanted his protection, and whatever influence his power could afford me: a dweller-turned-god navigating blindly through Topia. I was unsure of my place, and that uncertainty became so much more as I watched Willa with her Abcurses. I had poured blood, sweat and tears into advocating for the dwellers, into fighting for a better dweller lifestyle. I had died for my dweller cause, only to be brought back as a god.

What kind of twisted fate was that?

I tried to pull myself from my head, to listen as everyone filled Willa in on what had happened after we had both blacked out. Most of it I already knew, or had pieced together myself. Staviti was in love with Pica, Pica was obsessed with … everything—Rau and *Willy* especially. Staviti stopped his attack because he was outnumbered, and because Pica turned up. And now we were here, stuck with the Goddess of Insanity while Willa tried to swindle her way into a separate residence on the other side of the platform.

I followed along after them as we left the room and exited into one of Pica's chaotic gardens, listening in near-admiration as Willa carefully navigated the goddess's craziness. I supposed that Willa's own mother had prepared her quite adequately for dealing with the crazy mood-swings of an unbalanced woman. In no time at all, she had managed to convince Pica that it would be even *more* lovely if she lived separately, as far away from Pica's own residence as she could manage, without actually leaving the platform. As soon as Pica agreed, it was as though her craziness caught a whole new wind. She started planning right there on the spot.

"You *must* pick a colour-scheme, Willy," she announced. "I will fetch the best builder in Topia and he will build you something incredible, but you must pick your colours first."

Willa was nodding and the rest of us were grinning as Pica finally ran off in the direction that Willa had managed to convince her would be the perfect place to live.

"Do you think you will be safer with us, or with Cyrus?" Willa was serious now, turning her attention to me.

"Cyrus," I replied, before snapping my mouth shut. *What? What the hell!* I hadn't meant to say that.

"You're probably right," she replied, her forehead creasing as she tapped at her chin, apparently deep in thought. "We need to keep you hidden as much as possible ..."

She trailed off as Pica returned, striding out of her house with several waves of material flowing out behind her in a cascade of colours.

"How about lilac?" she asked, fanning out one of the sections of material, displaying the light purple colour.

"What is the lilac going to be for?" Willa asked, sounding a bit afraid.

"Everything!" Pica announced, glowing. "Once you pick a colour, you *must* commit! Loyalty is love, my dear. How about magenta? Orange? Topaz?"

I tried to mask my snort, but Willa heard it anyway, shooting me a narrow-eyed glare. I could tell that she was trying to figure out how to escape from Pica's decorating obsession, but I already knew that she had lost the battle.

FOUR

CYRUS

My limit had been reached.

"If I have to spend one more fucking click discussing colour schemes, I'm going to kill everyone on this platform," I announced.

Emmy just rolled her eyes in my direction.

Willa didn't even lift her head. "Stop being so dramatic Cyrus," she told me, her eyes still glued to all the fabrics sprawled across her lap. "I'm sure you don't have anything better to do."

I stopped my pacing—sitting still would definitely cause my energy to spiral free and annihilate something Pica loved, which would cause a shit-show I wasn't prepared to deal with. "Gods are not dramatic," I informed them. "We're powerful and commanding and we don't waste time on colou—"

Willa cut me off. "I'm not sure that I can commit that fully to one colour. I change my favourite colour every rotation." She held up a small swatch. "Plus, if I choose purple, Siret will gloat about it, and then Coen will throw him through a wall and then he'll throw Coen through a wall, and then Yael will have to throw someone through a wall because he won't be outdone, and then Rome will throw someone through a wall because everyone's smashing things … and then we'll have no walls. Nobody wants that."

"So, that rules out green, gold, purple, blue, and dark grey," Emmy reminded her, listing off the colours of Abil's sons.

Meanwhile, I hadn't missed the fact that both of them were ignoring me, completely unafraid of my current pissed-off state.

"No fucking respect," I muttered, turning my back on the pair and storming off because they were driving me insane.

The Abcurses had left some time ago in an attempt to ferret out friend and foe among the gods, which meant that I was stuck babysitting the two dweller-turned-gods in front of me. I'd had enough babysitting to last a lifetime, but at least Pica wasn't there. *A small blessing.* She had left Willa with all the colour schemes and a two-rotation time limit on deciding. We were nearing the end of her allotted time and Willa still hadn't decided on anything except that the Abcurse colours were eliminated, and that orange might be a hazard, because *how will she know if she's accidentally started another fire if she's surrounded by orange*? I had actually agreed with her on that point. I should have told them about what Pica did when someone didn't make their deadline, because Willa had committed herself to a strict deadline whether she realised it or not ... and Pica took commitment *very* seriously.

"Willa." Emmy used her reasonable voice: the soothing and convincing one. I had to ignore my urge to cover her mouth with my own and absorb the fire that filled her whenever she got bossy. "I think you should just go monochromatic. You can add your own splashes of personality after that—maybe something from all of the Abcurses' colours. And if you make the main decor black or white, you can change the accessories all the time. You'll never get sick of it."

I really was going to walk out this time.

"You're so smart, Emmy," Willa exclaimed. "All of the Abcurse colours together would be perfect." I knew they would be hugging again. "But I'm not sure I can go with black because of Death, or white because of ... reasons." They both turned and looked at me, and I just crossed my arms, shaking my head.

"You'd be lucky to have my colour," I told Willa. "Neutral is powerful. Untouchable. Pure. Original. Even more original than the very first gods."

"Uh huh," she said, her lips twitching. "It's amazing, Cyrus, truly one of a kind."

I stilled. "Are you mocking me?"

She flashed a grin in my direction. "Come on. White is a little boring, don't you think?"

Emmy chuckled, and that fired me up even more.

"No," I declared. "I do not think that at all. In fact, it's the best colour you could ever have, and if you don't choose white as your colour, I'm going to be really upset."

For fuck's sake. I needed to get out of there. Those two were turning me into a dweller. I was discussing interior colour schemes. *And why did I give a shit if they didn't like my colour*? The opinions of bugs shouldn't matter to me. It never had before.

A frustrated sound crept up from my chest, but before I could release it and tell the occupants of the room how much they were affecting me, I turned and thrust the door open, stepping out onto the main platform.

I didn't go far because it was still my responsibility to keep the pair safe, and despite the fact that I had driven the knife into Willa's chest and tortured my little bug on a sun-cycle basis, I never wanted to see either of them hurt. My intention all along had been to keep them safe. My intention had *always* been to keep them safe. With Willa, I was sure that it had something to do with the balance of the worlds, but with Emmy ... I wasn't sure about anything.

"Times up!" Pica trilled, appearing from somewhere close by. She was always *hovering*.

Not wanting the girls alone with her, I followed her back into the main room, having regained a little of my control. I just needed to hold out until Willa's protectors got back, and then I could return with Emmy to my cave. That was a concept that should have bothered me, because I didn't like anyone in my space ... touching my things ... annoying me.

It had been somewhat of a surprise when Emmy had declared that she was safer with me. Obviously there was no safer place in either world, but I hadn't expected her to *acknowledge* it. I'd expected her to run as fast from me as she could. Especially after my declaration about wanting everything from her. That had scared her, I'd seen it in her face.

But she hadn't run.

The dweller was stronger than I'd given her credit for. She was certainly far more intelligent than most of the gods I knew. And she had put up with Willa for many life-cycles. That took great mental and emotional fortitude.

"What colour scheme did you choose?" Pica crooned as she reached the pair, who were still on the bed surrounded by fabric. "The builders are on their way as we speak."

Emmy seemed to have confiscated the colours from Willa, and she thrust a scrap of fabric at the goddess now. I couldn't see what they had chosen because Pica whipped it away so quickly, and then it was gone.

"Amazing choice," she crooned. "It's the perfect, most lovely, most perfectly lovely colour I've ever seen. I'll have the work commence immediately."

She spun quickly, gliding from the room and muttering about abstract art and the shape of round walls.

"So, what did you choose?" I asked the pair.

"Nothing," Willa said with a smirk. "Emmy reminded me that it probably didn't matter what colour I chose, Pica would find a way to turn it into something crazy. Emmy is going to run damage control secretly with the builders."

I rested my gaze on Emmy, shaking my head just a little as an unexpected smile tilted up my lips. *She has the intelligence of a god.*

That thought grew stronger after it entered my head, until all I could think about was how strong and smart and stunningly beautiful the new goddess before me was. There wasn't a single bug-like thing about Emmy in that moment, and I wondered if the transition to god-hood was continuing for both her and Willa. Maybe it was a slower ascension when it wasn't done by Staviti.

"Do either of you know your powers yet?" I asked, startling them with my subject change. "Most gods would have some idea by now."

Willa shrugged. "All I know is that mine isn't Chaos."

"If you believe that the god from the imprisonment realm is your father, Willa, you might not have ever been a dweller," Emmy said, voicing the thought we'd all had since Willa came back from the land of death.

Willa's voice was strained, breaking as she replied: "I have no idea if he's really my father, or if it was wishful thinking on my behalf. I'm desperate for some answers ..."

"What about Donald?" I asked bluntly. "Have you figured out a way to return the portion of her soul that you brought back? Can you still hear her in your head?"

Willa nodded, her lips trembling. "Yes, but ... there's nothing normal about her thoughts. And I still haven't figured out if it's possible to return her soul. The Abcurses can't return mine ... so there's that."

We fell quiet as Pica returned with the builders. I caught Emmy's arm before she could hurry out of the room after Willa.

"You shouldn't show yourself to any of the other gods," I warned her quietly.

She frowned, but I could tell that she was thinking about it. I used the fact that she was deep in thought to my own advantage, pulling her a few inches closer while she was distracted, staring after Willa's retreating form.

"What am I supposed to do?" she finally asked, tilting her head up so that her eyes could catch mine.

I swallowed, letting my hand drop from her arm.

She wasn't allowed to look up at me like that, all helpless and confused.

"Am I supposed to just hide away in your white cave until everyone is ready to know about me? How can I protect Willa from there?"

"How can I protect you if you're here?" I returned, biting back the bad taste that accompanied the words. She wasn't allowed to separate herself from me, just like she wasn't allowed to make me feel things with her big, blinking eyes.

"You should figure that out, and quickly," she warned me. "Because I'm not going to stay hidden away in your secret little alcohol hovel for the rest of my life—"

"You're a god, now," I interrupted her. "There are no more life-cycles. You're already dead. Your life has already ended. Now, there is only eternity."

"I'm not going to spend *eternity* hiding away in your wine closet!"

She jerked away from me, temper finally sparking through her innocently confused expression, turning her into the fiery creature that I was more familiar with.

"I think I know something that might help." I held out my hand to her, but she only narrowed her eyes on it, before flicking the same suspicious look up to my face.

"You'll pull me off the platform," she predicted.

I nodded, still holding out my hand, though I was starting to grow impatient already. I had never had to actually cater to anyone before—man or woman, mortal or god.

"But I haven't decided if I want to go back to your cave." She folded her arms across her chest, tucking her hands firmly away.

"You ... just said ... earlier, to Willa." I was stumbling over my words, my offered hand curling into a fist.

"I was saying that so she wouldn't worry. She has enough to think about right now without also trying to protect me."

"You can't protect yourself, Emmanuelle. You need me."

"Maybe," she hedged, her chin tilting up stubbornly.

"Frustrating woman," I grumbled, striding up to her and wrapping my hands around her upper arms, drawing her up onto her toes and against my chest.

Those damn eyes were wide again, tiny hints of need swirling behind the blockage of *fuck off* that she was trying to muster. I turned on the spot, pulling her with me through a pocket. I held her weight against me as we landed, the grass soft beneath us. A forest rose high around us, soft purple flowers dotting the grass of the clearing we stood in. Emmy drew closer to me, instinctively driven to shield herself with my body.

"What is this place?" she asked, her tone quieter than usual.

"This is where Terrance lives. It's his magic that you're feeling. Don't worry, it can't actually harm you. His magic cloaks the gods with something he calls a *predator shield*. It communicates to his animals that we are not to be hunted."

"Hunted?" Her tone was no longer quiet, but tinged with a shrillness that had me biting back a smile.

She scrambled away from my chest, putting her back to me and turning about to examine every edge of the clearing slowly and carefully.

"Terrance is the—"

"Bestiary God," she supplied distractedly. "I know. Why are we here?"

"He is a little more ... *attuned* to the base nature of beings than most gods are," I explained, reaching out and wrapping my hand around a section of her robes.

I figured she wouldn't let me touch her to lead her forward in any way, so this would have to do. "We're going to ask him if he can tell us what your power is."

"I thought we weren't supposed to be showing me to outsiders?" she goaded, sticking close to my back as I picked my way through the trees.

The animals were gathering about us, but they stayed out of our way. I could feel the heat of their bodies close by, and hear the rustle of leaves along the ground.

"As a general rule, yes. But I have leverage over Terrance, and I don't have leverage over the builders."

"What leverage?" she asked, as we reached a small footbridge.

I didn't answer because Terrance himself had just emerged from the water beneath the bridge. His saturated robes were half pulled off, tied about his waist and draped in reeds. His green eyes were like the moss he loved to play in; his long, brown hair slicked back from his face.

"What leverage indeed?" he asked, his voice a whisper.

Emmy jumped, and then ground to a halt, her eyes riveted to the Bestiary God.

"How long will you lord that over me?" Terrance continued, walking toward us, his feet bare against the grass. "It was a harmless little prank."

"If Staviti ever found out that you and Pica had sex, he would make it his mission to end you just as he's made it his mission to end Rau," I reminded him. Leverage was the currency of the gods.

"I'm sorry," Emmy spoke loudly, stepping forward and holding up her hands, before addressing Terrance. "You slept with ... Pica? Pica who loves Rau to the point of creepy obsession?"

I could tell that she had paused to give Terrance a more thorough inspection, and I fought not to drag her back to my side. Especially when her eyes caught and lingered on his bare chest. Eventually she turned to me, her eyebrows arched.

The question in them was clear: Pica had once diverted her attention from Rau? And she *still* didn't want anything to do with Staviti, her own creator?

"Pica is a complicated goddess," Terrance drawled, coming to a stop a few feet away from Emmy. "She taught me everything I know about women."

"My congratulations to your lucky future partners," Emmy muttered dryly.

"We are not permitted partners," he returned

with a smile in her direction, though he glanced toward me at the last moment.

The bastard already knew that I wanted her.

"And yet Pica and Rau are together, and Abil and Adeline are together," Emmy returned, completely missing the hidden meaning behind his words.

"And countless others." Terrance waved his hand dismissively in the air. "As much as he tries to stop it, love is an epidemic, no matter which world you live in. Try as you might to cure it, another strain of the disease will always emerge. It seems to evolve beyond us, always one step ahead. Don't you think?"

Emmy didn't answer. Her jaw was set, her eyes hardened. It seemed he had already sensed something in her as well ... and she didn't like it.

FIVE

EMMY

Terrance was calm. His movements slow and smooth, his voice never rose above a certain octave. I figured this was because he created and lived with dangerous creatures for fun, but it was unnerving. I didn't like the feelings he brought about in me. I didn't like his words. They were a warning, clear and simple. He was warning me away from Cyrus, but Cyrus had already told me he wanted everything, so he clearly didn't want to adhere to Staviti's rule.

Cyrus had been with other women, that much I knew. So this sudden warning from Terrance was something more. This was about more than just sex. In general, it went against every one of my instincts to not respect rules, but if they didn't make sense—

logically—my mind would rebel. What reason did Staviti have for banning partners? Was it because Pica refused to love him? Maybe he had created the ban to separate Pica from Rau, but it had backfired, causing Pica to resent him and pull even further away from him. That would explain why he didn't explicitly try to enforce the rule. It had already backfired on him.

So why not remove the rule altogether?

I could only assume that if Staviti wasn't allowed to be with the person he wanted, then nobody else was allowed to be either.

"Don't move," Terrance suddenly whispered, and I found myself freezing to the spot, barely even allowing breath to wheeze out between my pursed lips. At first, I thought it was an attack of some sort. I waited for Staviti and his army to descend, but it didn't happen. I should have known better: Cyrus was far too calm. Willa had told me in a rushed whisper earlier how he'd reacted when I had died. Part of me couldn't quite believe he'd been so emotional, angry and vengeful. I wasn't sure why he had done it, but it stood to reason that if Staviti was about to attack again, Cyrus wouldn't be so casual.

"Hello, pretty girl," Terrance crooned—further

confirming that Staviti wasn't the one to disturb our meeting.

My eyes widened as a creature shuffled into view, standing up high on huge back legs to forage in the trees before dropping down with a heavy thump again. *Pretty girl?* Okay, sure. I guess if you thought five eyes, twelve spindly tentacles protruding from around her face, and a huge rotund furry body were all 'pretty,' then … sure.

"A boband," Cyrus explained to me, keeping his voice just as low as Terrance's. "They're very rare, living both on land and in water. They hold enough venom in one tentacle to kill twenty dwellers."

"Can they hurt a god?" I asked, curiosity getting the better of me as I got over her crazy appearance.

Terrance chuckled. It sounded oddly forced. "I would never allow my creatures to harm the gods, but … if Death were to collaborate on a project with me …" He trailed off, completely lost in thought as I grew increasingly more and more uncomfortable, until he finally blinked and returned to the original topic. "They can stay under water for fifty clicks without the need for air. Their poison will incapacitate a god for a short amount of time, but nothing on this world can actually kill a god. Except another god."

His eyes fluttered as he slowly turned to Cyrus. There was some sort of silent communication going on there, but I was too interested in the boband to pay close attention. The creature shuffled forward. It was on all four stocky legs now, its body almost as huge as the bridge beside Terrance. She lowered her face, the tentacles spreading out around her as she sniffed along the ground.

"They eat berries and swimmers, mostly," Terrance said, continuing his explanation. "And require a lot of food, so they're always scavenging."

"Why did you create her?" I asked, wanting to understand what drove the Bestiary God to fashion such creatures. "Does she have a purpose?"

Flashing eyes met mine. "All of my animals have a purpose, just because you cannot see it, doesn't mean it isn't there."

"So, what's her purpose?" I pushed, because he was giving me a half answer, and I didn't like those.

Terrance ignored me then, turning to face Cyrus. "Why are you here? What do you need from me?"

Cyrus swept out an arm and before I knew it, he had drawn me closer, into his side. I tried not to feel all of the warmth and energy that surrounded him constantly. I also tried not to lean into him.

I tried and failed, for the most part.

"I need you to tell me what sort of god Emmanuelle is." Cyrus got straight to the point.

Terrance stilled. "You don't know? Did Staviti not help you?"

Tension shot through Cyrus. "You already know the answer to that."

He didn't sound angry, but the other god was suddenly looking very wary, and he didn't ask anymore prying questions. He just stepped forward, slowly, until he stood right before me.

"Do I have permission to touch you?" he asked, staring intently into my eyes. The only sound in the clearing at that moment was the boband just snuffling along, sucking up berries as it foraged.

I swallowed hard. "Touch me where?"

You had to always clarify things with gods, they were sneaky bastards.

Cyrus chuckled next to me, and I was pretty sure he said *that's my girl* under his breath.

"Nothing untoward at all," Terrance assured me. "Just on your temples."

Since most of my brain was occupied with the possibility that Cyrus had called me his girl—*why did that excite me so much?*—I kind of lost focus and just nodded, giving Terrance the permission he sought.

His touch was gentle, but the skin on his hands was rough, scraping across my cheek bones as he settled both palms on either side of my face. "This shouldn't hurt," he said, as his hands began to heat.

"Those three words are in no way reassuring," I told him dryly. "I hadn't been expecting it to hurt, so now all you've done is make me worry that it will hurt."

Terrance chuckled. "You're an unusual female, I'll give you that. I can see the appeal."

"Mine," Cyrus ground out immediately, the word sounding like it had been forced from him. I blinked, twisting my head so I could see him better, because there was a guttural nature to that word.

He was glowing, a white light shining from his eyes and around his body, like a shimmery field. Terrance noticed this as well, and from the corner of my eye, I thought he went very pale. "Noted," he told Cyrus, voice rough. "I will say nothing more."

He was afraid of him, and suddenly I could understand why. Cyrus was in his Neutral state. The one everyone seemed to fear. But I refused to allow him to control me with fear.

Shaking Terrance's hands off, I spun toward Cyrus and elbowed him hard in the ribs. The impact caused my elbow to ache.

The god turned his glowing eyes on me. "Did you just ... hit me?" he asked, his voice still in that unnaturally low tone.

"Yes," I said loudly—I had no idea why I was shouting, I couldn't seem to stop myself. "Because you are so godsdamn annoying. Stop it. Right now. We are trying to figure out what sort of god I am, I don't need you to scare off the only being who might be able to tell us."

Cyrus looked stunned. He even shook his head a few times, as if he were trying to make sure his ears weren't malfunctioning. A bubble of laughter started to rise in my chest, and I tried to force it down, but he looked so damn confused. A snort escaped, and I bit my lip, but my chest was heaving as my amusement began to escape.

"Are you sure she's yours?" Terrance asked, his eyes locked on me. "Her spirit. It's wild ... like my creatures."

In the next click, Cyrus's hand was wrapped around Terrance's throat. "I'm not sure I can make myself any clearer," he snarled, his white light reaching a new level of blinding. My humour dried up then, and I wondered where I should hit him this time. "Don't even think about it," Cyrus rumbled over his shoulder. "Some gods will only learn through force. Terrance is clearly one of them."

"Right ... here," Terrance gasped out. "Mess ... message received."

"Can you just not kill him until we find out what sort of god I am?" I asked. "It's driving me crazy not knowing."

It really was. The unknown wasn't something I dealt well with.

In a huff, Cyrus dropped the other god and took a step closer to me. "You have five clicks," he said shortly.

Terrance dragged himself up, looking a little more ruffled than before. He rubbed at his throat, and I could see the dark marks already marring his skin.

"I have a pretty good idea already," he said, swallowing hard. "Especially after both of our reactions to her, but I want to confirm."

What did he mean by that? Their reactions to me?

This time, when his hands landed on my face, I locked my gaze on him. My eyes narrowed as I prepared myself for whatever pain was coming my way. The heat was immediate, and more intense than it had been last time. Clearly he was ready to get this over with so that we were no longer in his forest, irritating him ... or trying to choke him.

As his fingertips settled firmly against my skin, I heard the murmur of his voice. "Close your eyes, it will help you relax."

I thought that was bad advice, but I did it anyway, allowing my eyelids to close, my vision sinking into darkness.

"Wildness," Terrance muttered, louder this time. "It is in here, inherent, but also gifted. Some of it is unnatural. Her powers are raw—almost clumsy."

"Willa," I said, the feeling of laughter bubbling up inside me. "Of course she did a clumsy job turning me into a god."

"That's not what I meant," Terrance countered, and I felt the pressure of his hands increase, the surface of his skin vibrating with a low frequency of warm power. "Your gift has been clumsily given—not adhering to the usual precise pattern of Staviti's companions, or even those that have ascended to god-hood."

Pretty much what I'd said, but he clearly needed the last word.

"Am I not a proper god?" I asked suddenly, my voice growing faint. I could feel my invincibility and strength dribbling away already.

"You are most certainly a *proper* god," Terrance assured me. "Just as you are most certainly a different *type* of god. I would be interested to feel the mind of the other girl—the one who challenged Staviti, who brought you back to life. The birds carry whispers to me, you know."

"What whispers have they told you about Willa?" Cyrus asked.

"They say that she is a storm, come to wash through this land. And those of us who live here will be raised by the waters, or we will drown."

"Do you believe that?" I asked, keeping my eyes closed.

"I always believe my animals," he told me. "And you should, too. They are pure voices of the land—much purer than you or I."

"Even though you created them?" I asked.

"I only fashioned them," he explained. "My power can animate, but it is Topia that lends them magic. They absorb it from the land. You asked what their purpose is, and that is your answer. They are conduits of magic—receptacles of Topia, to do as Topia bids."

"It's funny," I muttered, almost to myself. "The gods all seem to have an element of creation. Pica creates obsession out of love; Abil and Siret create things out of thin air; Coen creates pain; Yael creates will, where a person might be inclined otherwise; Aros creates desire; Rome changes the physics of his environment to have physical dominion over everything; and Willa ... she has created a new life. If you think about it in that way, you are all Creators."

"Of course." Cyrus was the one to answer me, and he sounded almost impressed. He was quiet for a moment more, before he spoke again. "Most of the gods are a product of Staviti, so their powers naturally take on a form that is in some way related to his magic. Those gods who ascended as he did have all gained lower forms of his Creation power, and that is probably because they are reaching Topia in the same way as he did. Frivolity, music, wine, fury, archery—there are many lesser forms of Creation, many lesser Gods, all manifesting their own creations in their own ways."

"And then there is you," Terrance interrupted, drawing his hands away from my head.

I blinked my eyes open, fixing them on him. He was staring at me, a slightly puzzled expression on his face.

"I can sense wildness, life, love, desire, nurturing ... all of these things, but I do not know *exactly* what your power is. I cannot tell you what kind of God you are."

"Is there any other way I can find out?" I tried to keep the disappointment out of my tone, not wanting to be rude. He had tried to help.

"Powers are often activated under duress." He took several steps away, and then turned his back on us, walking over to the bridge. "I think Neutral will be far better at raising your emotions than I, so I will leave that task to him. Good luck, Sister of the Storm."

SIX

CYRUS

Sister of the Storm? The fact that someone else had given her a nickname annoyed me, but I tried to keep the annoyance off my face as I gripped Emmy's arms and pulled her into me. She didn't have time to ask any of the many questions that were undoubtedly trying to spring from that busy mind of hers before we were standing in a clearing.

"Have we left Beastiary's forest?" she asked, quickly pushing away from me and turning on her heel to take in the space.

"We are close to my home," I replied. "I thought it would be better if we did this here, away from ... Donald."

"What is *this*?" she asked, immediately turning again, her eyes narrowing sharply. "You better not put me under any kind of *duress*, you Sacred Asshole—"

"I won't need to," I said, quickly cutting her off. "You constantly put yourself under duress. I'm only going to sit here and witness it while I wait for something to happen."

With those words, I sized up a comfortable-looking boulder, settling back against it, folding my arms. Her mouth was hanging open, her face falling into confusion.

"You're going to just ... wait until it happens?"

"That's right." I grinned. "Neither of us is leaving this forest until something happens. There's a cave just through the trees behind you. We can sleep there if the need arises, and a small stream just a few paces behind me if there's need of privacy."

"You're in need of a sanity check," she mumbled, dropping to sit cross-legged on the grass. "This is never going to work, and it's definitely not going to put me under duress."

"Then I also won't speak to you." My smile was growing. I couldn't help it. "With nobody to talk to, nobody to answer your questions, and no way out of this forest, I believe you will very quickly lose your temper."

She spluttered out some more insults, before

letting out a huff, getting to her feet, and storming off. I was powerful enough to feel her energy, even when she was out of sight. So I didn't move. I let her go and she stomped around, no doubt trying to calm the cluttered mess her mind was in.

My mind was troubled as well. Terrance had been less useful than I had expected, and far more frustrating. Seeing him touch Emmy shouldn't have bothered me, but ... it did. And it wasn't just the touching but also his fascination with her. Terrance loved to collect things—his animal creations, the most beautiful parts of nature, and the strongest of allies.

It was in his personality to build a secure nest and to fill it with all of his favourite things. I'd be damned if Emmy ended up as one of those things.

"This isn't going to work," she announced, bursting back into the clearing. "I'm telling you right now, this sort of environment isn't the right one for me discover a new power. I need books. Order. A quiet, tidy place to gather my thoughts."

I almost laughed, because that sounded exactly like my cave. *We matched.* Her energy drew me, and I stood so I could stalk closer to her. My focus remained locked on her like she was my prey. I didn't do it because I wanted to scare her, but because I couldn't look away. Her eyes grew very wide, and even though she didn't seem to want to, she started to back up slowly. Something unfurled inside my chest—a need to pursue her until she submitted to me. Until she gave me exactly what I wanted.

"Why are you looking at me like that?" she asked, curiosity and fear warring in her tone.

She stopped moving when her back hit a nearby tree. I stopped as well. "Come to me," I said. "Stop fighting it, because you know you'll eventually give in."

Her cheeks went pink, and I smiled. It was when she was riled up that her power shone the brightest.

"You're so arrogant," she said, stepping forward suddenly. Her finger came out so that she could jab me in the chest. I barely felt it, but it still amused me that she was so relaxed about trying to injure me. "You don't own me, and I'll never submit to you."

I moved with extra speed, her finger and hand in mine in a micro-click. Emmy paused, the words dying on her tongue.

"Are you sure?" I whispered, leaning down closer to her. "You're so tightly wound. Don't you wish there was someone in the worlds you could rely on? Someone you could relax with and trust to catch you when you finally let yourself go free? No more rules and responsibilities. No more stresses."

I could be that god for her.

"You think you're the one I should trust?" she breathed, her lips trembling. "The very god who has such massive trust issues that he lives under the ground in a secret, warded cave?"

I shifted, feeling somewhat uncomfortable. It wasn't something I was used to, the way she could carve right to the truth.

"Neutral is alone. That's the nature of my power," I admitted, unsure why I was being so honest with her. "It's the only way I can remain impartial."

"You don't seem that impartial with me," she said, tilting her head back. The curve of her neck in that moment was so tantalising that I barely managed to not lean down and press my lips to it.

You're different, I thought, but I didn't say it out loud. "Maybe we should explore the area?" I suggested, finding that I was the one who needed some breathing room.

She was ... a lot. Too much. *Everything.*

Emmy nodded, not fighting me for once. "Sure, show me this damn cave we'll sleep in if I don't discover my powers before then."

"Terrance was right," I murmured, not expecting her to hear me.

She did though—of course she did. "Right about what?"

I wanted to lie because I was giving her too much power, but I found myself again telling her the truth. "You're filled with fire and life. You are unique." *Special.*

Her face crumbled for a moment, before she recovered, sniffling and sucking in a deep breath. "Did you know my parents died when I was young? A sickness went through our town, and they both fell ill almost straight away. I barely remember them, I was so young, but there is one thing I do recall with almost perfect clarity."

She spoke matter-of-factly, but I sensed the sadness seeping from her as she continued.

"My mum always tucked me in at bedtime. She would wrap my blanket tightly around me because I was afraid of sleepers getting in, and she would say the same thing to me every single time. 'You might be born a dweller, but you can still rise up. You can be the best dweller there is. Always remember: you are loved ... you are perfect ... you are unique.'"

She swallowed, and I fought against the urge to pull her closer to me. Seeing such strong emotion on her face was bothering me, and I wanted to comfort her, but I knew she wasn't done.

"After they died, I had nowhere else to go. Willa's mum took me in because she was the only one who really didn't care about another dweller being in her house. The first night there, I waited for her to put the blankets tightly around us. But she wasn't even there to say goodnight. It was just me and Willa."

"And that's how it's been since then?" I finished.

Emmy nodded. "Yes." She looked around then, her eyes hazy. "I had forgotten about that until you called me unique. Subconsciously though, I think it's part of the reason I've always strived to be the best dweller. Top of my station."

"Your mum loved you," I said. "She wanted you to know that what you were born as does not define you."

"And yet, it always has."

I shook my head. "No, it hasn't. I have been watching you since Willa was first brought to my attention, and in all of that time, you have acted like a dweller in only one way. You cared about other dwellers. In all other ways, you have acted with the confidence, strength, and resilience of a sol. And now that you are a god ... I think that you will be one of our greatest."

"One of your greatest?" she parroted, apparently shocked. She started laughing, then. *Okay, she was definitely shocked*. "One of your greatest!" she repeated, laughing harder.

She eventually threw up her hands, and then settled them against my chest, roughly trying to push me back. I didn't budge, but I smirked at the effort she had put into it.

"Well, we know one thing for sure..." I murmured, ducking my head to force her eyes to mine.

As soon as I caught her attention, she lifted her chin stubbornly, refusing to look away—as I knew she would.

"What's that?" she asked.

"Your ability certainly isn't Strength," I remarked.

She scowled, shoving against my chest again. Her cheeks were growing pink. She had thought that I was making fun of her with my earlier comment, I could tell. I curled my fingers beneath her chin, forcing her head up even further as I straightened a little.

"I meant it, Emmanuelle. I have seen the rise and fall of many gods—because as you've discovered, they aren't as invincible as they seem—and I know greatness when it's standing in front of me."

I ducked down again, pressing my lips to hers before she could stop me. She gasped a little—either from my statement or my sudden kiss, I wasn't sure. I pressed harder against her soft mouth, my fingers moving from her chin to the base of her neck, before threading into her hair.

She melted the same way she did every time I kissed her, but I knew that she would grow stiff as a board the micro-click that I pulled away. I would have to watch the iron shutters fall into place over her eyes. I would have to watch that delicious mouth firm into a hard line again. I couldn't bear to see the change, so I deepened the kiss. I pushed my tongue into her mouth, my hands finding her shoulders before dipping down over the curve of her spine. I could feel every inch of her through the robes, and my hands hooked around her thighs by instinct, pulling her up and drawing her legs around my waist. She followed like she had been made to fit me, to complement me, to melt into me.

A sound from behind us threatened to distract me as I lost myself in the feel of her body arching up against mine, her tongue responding to me so sweetly. I pulled back slightly, the sound repeating itself, piercing through the fog that had descended over my mind.

"Oh my gods," Emmy muttered, sounding horrified. "Cyrus, put me down. Look."

I refused to release her, but I followed her pointed finger to look over my shoulder. Shock stole through me, loosening my hold on her. She found her feet and I quickly turned, pushing her behind my back.

A line of eight servers stood before us, each of them holding a small axe. Their eyes were glowing with colour—a hint of blue mixed with a hint of red, swirling around a pearly white orb. One of them pulled his arm up and hurled his axe without warning, sending it *thudding* into the trunk of the tree only a few inches to the right of us.

"Stop," I ordered, reaching over to pull the axe free. I had a feeling I was about to need it. "You have just attacked a god."

They didn't reply. They advanced—three steps, in unison. One of them let out a strange, mechanical groaning sound.

"They're in pain," Emmy whispered into my back.

"There's something wrong with them," I returned, raising my axe hand and focusing on the servers. "Stay back," I ordered, injecting some of my power into the words. "Or I will be forced to shut each of you down."

In reply, another of the servers threw her axe. I battered it away with my own, re-directing it to the ground a few feet away. Another two axes followed in quick succession, and I knocked each of those away while I raised my other hand, my fingers spread out, power rushing to fill my entire body before exploding out of my extended reach.

The light that filled the clearing would have been overwhelming for Emmy, so I turned and pulled her face against the front of my robes. As my energy hit the servers, I felt a strong clash—my deadly light slamming into a barrier much tougher than any server should have possessed, but still, they were defeated. Their energy waned, and their vessels exploded. I held Emmy where she was, not wanting her to see the ashes that would remain behind. I definitely wanted to put her under duress, but not the kind of duress that she would never forgive me for, and I doubted that my 'they were going to kill us' excuse would work.

As the light finally filtered away, I began to move Emmy in the direction of the cave, but both of our feet stalled when a small, mechanical groaning sound floated over to us.

What the fuck? *It wasn't possible.*

I turned, shock and disgust slamming through me in equal measure. The creatures were ... putting themselves back together. The specks and pieces that should have been piles on the ground were floating back into place, fitting into now-grotesque-looking faces and figures. Emmy made a noise that indicated she was about to be sick, and I quickly grabbed one of the fallen axes, pushing it into her hands.

"Run," I ordered, pointing ahead of us. "Get to the cave."

For once, she didn't argue with me.

SEVEN

EMMY

Staviti knew about me and was trying to kill me. That was the only thing that made sense. Why else would he create indestructible servers, and then send them right to Cyrus and me?

Or was he trying to kill Cyrus?

Was Cyrus even killable? There was a definite grey area with the gods and death. Even being sent to the imprisonment realm was a form of death, although ... Willa had returned. There was a way for souls to come back from that world and re-inhabit the vessels that they had left behind.

"What the hell are you thinking about now?" Cyrus growled as he pushed right behind me, forcing my legs to move faster and my mind to focus.

"Things aren't adding up," I huffed. "With this

entire world. With the gods. I've thought so for a long time, but I was taught to just accept whatever stories I heard of your kind. I've never allowed myself to explore all the inconsistencies."

"Until now," Cyrus said, sounding amused and annoyed. An emotion he did particularly well.

Cyrus distracted me when he placed his hand on my back. He then gently pushed me into the mouth of the cave, darkness closing in around us. He spun as soon as we were inside, waving his hand in a half-arc and sending white light out. The light began to knit itself together in a circular pattern. Very quickly, the entrance to the cave was barred to all murderous servers.

"That should keep them out," he said as I laid down my axe. "At least until we can figure out what's going on here and how we're going to stop them from going about their little maiming spree."

It was darker now that the entrance was covered, the webbed barrier dimming down to an almost-solid blackness, though light seemed to shine around Cyrus without him doing anything, giving us just enough visibility. The cave was small, about twenty feet around, and unless there was a tunnel further back in the darkness—which I was pretty sure there wasn't—we were trapped in there until Cyrus removed his barrier.

While I had been exploring our surroundings, Cyrus had been watching me. He remained in the same position, doing his scary glowing thing. "What were you thinking before?" he asked. "About things not adding up?"

I was surprised that he hadn't just pushed that from his mind ... almost like he needed to know my thoughts.

"There are just a lot of inconsistencies. Like ... that story about Staviti's beginnings. How he came to be the Original God. Dwellers and sols are all taught the same story: that he was sick as a child, his father was a miner and found special water, and it healed his son and gave him extra abilities. Staviti then went on and had a bunch of children, creating sols and so on. But ... Willa didn't see that history in the Mortal Glass. She saw something completely different. Which version is true?"

He stilled then, and everything inside of me froze because in that stillness was a predator, waiting to kill. "The Mortal Glass ..." he said slowly, letting the word trail off. There was a long pause and then: "The glass never lies."

Which meant ... "Staviti lied," I breathed. "About

his origin story. How the hell did he manage that? Did he kill everyone who knew the truth?"

And why? Why would he lie about it? What was he trying to hide?

"What story did Willa see in the glass?" Cyrus asked me, still holding himself with unnatural stillness. "When did she tell you this?"

I hesitated, unsure if I was supposed to share it with anyone else. It was Cyrus though, and despite everything that had happened—despite him being a god—I trusted him. "She told me that Staviti was the son—a twin actually—of the last royal couple in Minatsol. That the Queen was pregnant, but she was sick, so they found a local person who knew how to get into Topia. She had her twin boys in the waters of Topia, saving them all—herself and both of her babies. Her sons were changed in the process."

"Staviti had a brother? Another just like him? There is no way." Cyrus blinked.

I nodded at him. "It's true. The god from the imprisonment realm—the one Willa thinks might be her father—is Staviti's twin. Which means technically, he would have the same powers as Staviti. They were both changed in the same way, in almost the same instant. He was the oldest, the one who would have inherited the crown." Only ... the royal ascension had died off after Staviti's parents. Whatever happened, whatever Staviti did, it changed the entire governing system of Minatsol.

"The last king of Minatsol was a miner," Cyrus said suddenly. "The Queen was the one of royal blood: she met and married the love of her life."

I blinked at him slowly, trying to figure out how the hell he knew that.

He shrugged, reading my expression. "I have a lot of time on my hands to read. There aren't a lot of things I don't know."

In that moment, he was twenty times hotter than he'd ever been. Intelligence did it for me. His was teamed with arrogance as well, but that was kind of to be expected for a god.

"So, Staviti only lied about some parts of the story."

Cyrus's barrier across the entrance swelled toward us slightly, and it looked as though several more of the servers had appeared and were trying to get in.

"It'll hold," he told me, catching my worried expression. "Staviti's brother ... what was his name?"

It was almost like Cyrus thought things through in the same way I did. Piecing together the random facts to make a whole picture.

"Jakan. Do you think he's in the imprisonment world because Staviti was trying to cover up his past? Is there a way to ask him, to go back there somehow the way Willa did?"

Cyrus wrapped his hands around my biceps, firm, but not hurting me. He drew me closer and up, so that my feet almost left the ground. I swallowed roughly because it looked as though he wasn't about to offer up an answer to my question, which meant that I had angered him by hinting that I might try to get into the imprisonment realm. To distract him from what I had said, I started speaking again. "What does it mean for Willa if Jakan is her father?"

His expression barely changed. "It would explain a lot," he eventually said, taking on a faraway look in his eyes. It was almost like he'd forgotten that he held me up. "As the daughter of a creator, she might have inherited some kind of godhood from him ... but, she also must be half dweller, to be the way she was originally—before her death. A body not strong enough to house her power. It was supressed within her, only escaping to cause small amounts of chaos in her life."

It did make sense.

"The only part that I don't understand," he said, finally focussing on me again, "is how he managed to get Willa's mother pregnant, when he has clearly been stuck in the imprisonment world since before Staviti first 'appeared' as a god."

A noise from beyond the barrier halted our conversation, and I glanced toward the woven barrier. Through it, we could now see that servers had lined up outside the cave; they watched us, completely unmoving. Unless you counted the unnatural tilt in their postures from having somehow pieced their bodies back together. It was as though they couldn't replicate the same bodies as before—as though they couldn't find the same balance, the same exact place for their parts. One of the man's eyes had been switched around, making it almost dizzying to try and look at him. Another woman had somehow reconstructed her arms so that one was significantly shorter than the other. Her ears were now also double the size of a normal pair of ears.

"I think there's a lot we still need to learn about Topia," Cyrus murmured, almost to himself.

I glanced over at him: he was watching the servers too, a deeply pensive look on his face.

"And a lot we still need to learn about Staviti," I added.

"They are one and the same." He waved his hand

at the cave wall again, but this time the rock began to shift, cracking and groaning until a large slab of it crawled across the entrance, blocking out both the barrier and the waiting servers.

We were thrown into an even deeper darkness, but it was only temporary, as tiny little white lights began to flicker into being, crawling along the walls of the cave and settling into small nooks and crevices. The entire cave was visible now, and I walked along to the back wall, running my hands along the rough stone, my fingers catching in all the uneven places. Cyrus watched me. We were both too deep in thought to snap at each other the way we usually did.

"Why are we hiding in here?" I eventually spoke up. "Can't we just go through a pocket, back to your home?"

He laughed, but there was a flash of something defiant in his bright eyes. "Nice try, bug. I told you: we're not leaving until you display your power. Even if it means we're trapped in a cave while an army of altered servers builds up outside."

I growled, the angry sound vibrating from the cave walls. "You're the all-powerful, gods-dammed Neutral, why can't you just ... force it out of me?"

"I'd much rather wait until you can no longer

contain it." He smirked. "I like the thought of watching you come undone, of being the one to witness the mess I know you have somewhere inside of you."

"There is no mess inside of me." I sniffed. "I clean and organise whatever is inside me several times a sun-cycle. I would never leave a mess, even where nobody can see it."

He rolled his eyes and held a hand out, stretching his fingers as a small sphere of spidery, contained light flickered into existence, arching toward his skin as though eager to dive back inside him. I backed away from the evil, expectant glint in his eyes.

"What are you doing?" I narrowed my eyes on him, feeling my way along the wall. I was cornered, no matter where I moved.

"Raising your emotions," he replied. "I thought we'd start with fear."

"And then?" My hand caught against a loose rock wedged into the cave wall. I pulled it behind my back as Cyrus stalked toward me.

"And then pain," he answered, looking as though he was a micro-click away from tossing that ball of white light at me.

I acted first, hurling the rock toward him. He

flicked it away without even blinking. I remained where I was standing, rage starting to swell inside me. I hated being cornered.

"Fine!" I finally shouted, holding both of my hands up. He lowered his arm an inch. I stepped toward him, and then held my arm out.

"You can hit me here." I pointed to my forearm. "We'll see if pain works."

He stared at my arm, and then stared at me. Eventually, he snorted. "That isn't pain."

"It is for a dweller."

"You're a god."

"I was a dweller a moon-cycle ago. It still counts. I'm sure my brain is wired to react just the same as when I was a dweller. It hasn't had time to settle into my new invincibility yet."

He rolled his eyes up toward the roof of the cave, exasperated, before sighing out, "Fine."

I screwed my eyes shut, preparing for him to punch my arm, but his fingers wrapped around my wrist instead. I blinked one eye open. He was staring at my forearm, his other hand finding the sleeve of my robe, brushing it up to my elbow to reveal my skin. I watched him as he watched me, staring too intently at my skin. He pushed the sleeve up higher, but the fabric bunched, refusing to go any further.

He made a frustrated sound, and the fingers around my wrist tightened, yanking me forward a step until the heat of his body was right there before me, burning down my front.

"You feel so full of *life*," he breathed out, almost in a trance, his hands moving to the neckline of my robes, fingers fanning out beneath the fabric, settling in against the bare skin of my shoulders with a heaviness that seemed possessive, almost needy. "What is this change?"

"The change would be that I died," I replied dryly, though my heart was suddenly beating so loudly that it almost drowned out my own words. "So I think you're picking up on the wrong *feeling* there."

"No, that's what it is," he rumbled against the top of my head, pulling me even closer so that I was now pressed fully along the front of his body.

His hands inched further out along my shoulders, pushing the robe out with the movement. I swallowed, my throat suddenly dry, my body starting to shake. "I don't know what you're talking about." This time, my reaction showed in my tremulous tone.

"Your skin is fucking vibrant," he answered. "You are starting to show your power, Emmanuelle."

EIGHT

CYRUS

The white light that formed the basis of my energy liked her. It was vibrating ... seeking out whatever power lay within Emmy. The longer I touched her perfect skin, the more difficult it was for me to not keep touching her. To not shift her robes away completely so than I could touch and taste every inch of her. She watched me with wide, wary eyes. But not with the level of fear I would have expected. In fact, she hadn't tried to back away from me—or push me away from her—since I started touching her, which was unexpected.

Something was shifting between us, and my Neutral energy definitely liked her.

So did I.

Before I could think it through, I was pulling her

into me. She lifted herself onto her toes, like she'd been waiting for me to make the move. Our lips met. The moment she opened her mouth, a rumble rocked through my chest. *Mine.*

Normally I would question the instinct that was rearing inside of me, the feeling that this woman in my arms was the only one that I was ever going to want in my world. But I was beyond questioning anything. All I wanted was this moment with her.

She pressed closer to me, making small throaty sounds. My hands slid down her body, along the shiny smooth robes, before I cupped my hands under her. She was tiny compared to most gods, weighing nothing as I lifted her up into my body.

She didn't fight me, but she also didn't wrap herself around me that way I'd seen Willa do with Abil's sons. It was like Emmy didn't know what to do with her legs, so she left them dangling there.

Or maybe she was too distracted, because our kiss was moving past the hot stage straight into an inferno.

"Cyrus," she gasped, wrenching her face from mine. "What are you doing?"

I took my time answering her, preferring to press my lips to her jaw first. Between each kiss I said, "I'm ... unlocking ... your ... power."

She groaned. "But you said pain ... I'm..."

Her words trailed off like she'd completely forgotten what she was going to say, and I grinned against her skin. Having her flustered was a novel experience; I liked that I was capable of making her lose control.

"Cyrus," she said again. There was something different in her tone and I paused, before lifting my head so that I could see her. "I'm glowing," she finished, her eyes wide.

I'd thought it was from me, the white light—even though it was unusual for me to lose control of it, even in such highly charged, emotional situations. But she was right: the glow that filled the room wasn't coming from me at all. It was hers.

"Am I like you?" she asked, swallowing hard. "Could I be another Neutral?"

I shook my head. "No, you don't have my power. I'm certain."

She hadn't been born of Topia; she didn't hold the same power. She was something different to me.

Her body arched slightly and the light filtering from her skin increased. And increased again. Within a click the room was so bright that anyone who wasn't a god would have been blinded from the light.

"Emmanuelle," I said slowly. "What are you doing?"

She didn't answer immediately, and worry edged through my mind—such a foreign emotion that it actually took me a moment to figure out that's what I was feeling.

"Emmy!" I repeated, with more force.

"Cyrus, I think this is my power."

My eyes were burning from the light, forcing me to close them. "You're a lightning bug?" I asked sarcastically, trying to figure out what I was supposed to do now.

"No," she answered, her voice huskier than I'd heard before. "I feel it now. I know exactly what my energy is ... I'm life. Creation. *Fertility*."

I stilled before slowly lowering her to the ground. She let out a low laugh, and then slowly the light faded away. My eyes adjusted immediately, and I blinked more than once, wondering if what I was seeing was possible.

"Fertility," I echoed back her previous word. "That's one way to put it."

The entire inside of the cave floor was now filled with plants and flowers and vines. Emmy had managed to bring an entire garden to life with her light. She could create life where there was nothing but emptiness.

"Do you know what this means?" she asked, breaking through my train of thought. I pulled my eyes from the lush flowers sprouting at our feet, lifting them to the stunningly beautiful goddess before me.

"What does it mean?"

She smiled. "It means that I have the power to bring life back to Minatsol. To the dead lands beyond the furthest rings. I can return everything that has been stolen from my home."

It annoyed me that she still thought of Minatsol as her home. I wanted her to feel that way about Topia, but I couldn't exactly blame her. Staviti was going out of his way to make everyone feel like they were in the middle of a war.

"We definitely need to keep you from Staviti now," I told her, my tone grave. "He hasn't allowed any children to exist in Topia. Only Abil's Trickery was able to finally defeat his determination to keep children out of this land. Not even Pica was allowed to keep her child."

"I thought he always loved Pica," Emmy said, surprised.

I shrugged. "He loved her so much that he wouldn't allow her to have a child with another."

Emmy froze, and I knew that her brain was immediately processing what I'd said and had reached a conclusion. "Staviti can't have children?" she asked me.

"No," I told her. "Pica told me once that it was his greatest desire. Whatever happened to make him into a god caused infertility. He can create gods, but no biological children."

"That's why," she breathed, shaking her head. "That's why he won't let the gods have or keep their children, he's angry that he doesn't have any of his own."

"That might be one reason," I allowed. "But it might also be a fear that any other beings born into godhood the way he was will only pose a threat to his power and rule."

She was worrying a finger against her lip as she sank deep into thought about something, and I took that moment to turn away, discreetly adjusting myself so that my obvious erection was a little less ... obvious.

Fertility.

Just what I needed. Emmy's power was forcing every molecule of my being to crave something that I had *already* been craving. I had a feeling that my life was about to get much more difficult.

"Can you put it away so I can think?" I finally growled at her, as I watched her pacing slowly back and forth in thought.

She paused, and her eyes widened. She quickly stepped into my space, and I cringed at the worry in her features. She wasn't using her power on me. I realised it before she even opened her mouth.

"Never mind," I grumbled, cutting across her words. "Let's get back to my home."

I pulled her into me, stepping us through a pocket and into my bedroom. I had intended to bring her into the lounge, but my thoughts had been distracted at the last click. I took some secret satisfaction in the heat that she tried to shield from her eyes as she quickly stepped away from me, casting a glance toward the mattress strewn across the debris on the floor.

Fuck it, I decided, moving over to the door.

"Donald!" I shouted.

"Yes, Sacred Ass—"

"Don't even think about calling me that again," I cut across her, as she appeared before me.

She quickly prostrated, her apologies raining down over me. Emmy or Willa would have pulled her up. I allowed her to grovel before I finally spoke.

"Go to the other side of the cave. Don't return until I call you, I can't have any more interruptions, am I clear?"

"Yes, Sacred One!" Donald jumped up, quickly hurrying off, and I waited until she was out of sight before closing and locking the door.

I didn't really need to lock it—but the click of the mechanism falling into place had the desired effect on Emmy. She started to back away from me, her expression becoming alarmed.

"W-what are you doing?" she stammered out.

"I helped you discover your power. Don't forget our deal. I agreed to help you, but in exchange I want you. I've been helping you since that promise, but now it's time for me to start collecting."

She stopped moving immediately, and I was sure that she even stopped breathing. Her fists were clenched by her sides, and to anyone who wasn't me, she would have looked furious ... but I knew better.

"What will you give me?" I asked her, as she battled with her needs.

She needed me, I could see that in the pooling of desire that had flooded into her gaze. Unfortunately, she also needed to be as stubborn as possible.

"What do you want?" I could tell that she wished to take back the question almost as soon as she voiced it, but I wasn't going to let that happen.

I quickly closed the space between us, my fingers gripping her robe, pulling on the loose material. Her slender figure was easy to make out as I tugged the material to the side, stretching it over her shape before releasing it to flutter back into place against her skin.

"Take this off," I ordered. "I want to see you glow."

I waited for her reaction, knowing very well that I had asked a very steep price for my first repayment from her. I was sure that she would throw something at me, or yell at me for ordering her around, but she didn't. She thought about it, her eyes holding mine steadily. I wasn't delusional enough to think that she was grateful to me; she was still pissed that I had locked us inside a cave, threatening to wait as long as it took to discover her power. After several clicks, she began to tug on the ties of her robe. My legs were suddenly weak, but I took a moment to send my power out and repair the bed and most of the furniture. I'd left it that way as a punishment of sorts, but it was time for all of us to heal.

Striding across the room to where she stood, my

hands found the sides of her face, my fingers gripping her firmly, but gently—turning her face up to meet mine. I kissed her curiously, tasting her need for me, feeling her short breaths against my mouth, the flushed skin of her face beneath my fingers, and hearing the breathy sounds she made whenever she thought I was about to pull away. I needed to assure myself that while I *was* coercing her ... she wasn't unwilling. I was never going to stop ordering Emmy around, just as I was never going to stop pushing her boundaries. She existed to test me, so it was only fair to test her back, but I had an innate fear of pushing her too hard, too fast. She had lived her life as a dweller, which made her more fragile than the sols who trained their whole lives to bear the possible burden of immortality and magic. I was afraid that by pushing Emmy too far, I would break her in some way.

The kiss grew desperate in a matter of moments, her hands pulling at my shoulders, my hands shaping to her ass. I had to keep reminding myself not to break her. When both of us were panting, I stepped back, walking backwards until the post at the end of my newly formed bed hit my back. Emmy stood there with rubbed red lips and tousled hair, her robes askew.

Yes, now she looked like she wanted what I was asking of her.

"The robe," I reminded her, my words almost a groan.

Gods, what has this woman turned me into?

NINE

EMMY

For the first time in my life, logic failed me. Because being with Cyrus was probably the worst decision I could make. On paper. If I was making a checklist about the pros and cons, the top of that list would be that he was not the sort of being —*god*—that one settled into a relationship with. And I was the relationship type. He was also controlling, powerful, domineering, and argumentative.

On the other hand, he was kind and smart and caring. He'd shown that ... in his own way, more than once. I did trust him, as much as anyone can trust a god.

And, all logic aside, Cyrus made me burn. He made my body come to life in a way that probably should have been illegal, because when he touched me, there was literally nothing he could ask that I wouldn't give him.

And I was about to give him exactly what he wanted: everything.

My robes fluttered almost silently to the floor; my breath caught in my throat because it was a vulnerable position to be in with someone like Cyrus. It was hard to truly let all of my guard down.

The silver of his eyes almost looked to be swirling as they ran across me. He took his time, starting at the top of my tousled blond hair and ending at the slippers I still wore. By the time he was done with that perusal, I was on fire. My skin was so sensitive that even the slide of my fingertips across my side as I moved was enough to send tingles through my body. Was this part of his power? Could he seduce me with one look? Sounded more like something that Aros would do, but whatever Cyrus was up to, he almost had me to the point of begging.

Swallowing against the dryness in my throat, I tried to keep my breathing steady. He reached out a hand and everything inside of me tensed in anticipation of the first touch. His palm pressed against the bare skin on my chest, just above the swell of my breasts. The heat was intense, branding.

I swallowed again, closing my eyes and allowing myself to not think. To just feel.

"Cyrus," I breathed.

I had no idea what I was asking him, I just needed him to do something.

His hand started to move down, slowly stroking, gently caressing my skin. It slid lightly across my bra, and then firmer over my stomach. He traced my curves like he was memorising them, and I started to panic that my legs were no longer going to hold me up.

"Do you want this?" he asked in a low rumble, leaning even closer to me.

My head was nodding before he even finished his question. "Yes, but no more teasing."

Cyrus's laugh was deep, and I lost the battle with my weak knees. One of his arms wrapped around me before I could stumble, pulling me tighter into his chest. I sucked in deeply, breathing him in. His scent was unlike anything I'd ever experienced before. It was like the crisp morning air right before a snow storm. It was so rare in Minatsol now to have rain and snow, but I remembered it from when we were kids. Once or twice a life-cycle, the snow would fall, and the rotations before that I always knew it was coming.

Snow was a lot like Cyrus, actually. White. Clean. Cold. Beautiful. So beautiful that it felt like the world turned into fantasy land when it fell, hiding the ugliness below. But it could also be deadly if you were caught out without proper protection.

Cyrus swung around suddenly, his arm still banded behind my back, lifting me as he walked toward the bed. He had used his power just before to repair his room, and the bed was now an impressive four-posted wood number. Carved. Ornate. I really didn't care, as long as we had a soft surface. Or any surface.

Nerves made themselves known in my gut as he laid me back, but the desire was so much stronger that I simply reached up and pulled his head down to mine. My body moved against his because there was no way I could stay still. Not anymore. I had to feel every part of Cyrus against me. I needed it. When he pulled back, lifting his head so that our eyes could meet, I almost groaned. His hair was tousled, his eyes wild, and he was glowing.

"You're glowing too," he murmured, and I wondered if I'd somehow mentioned his glow out loud. "I'm not sure I'll ever get enough of seeing your skin like this."

He was touching me again, holding himself up

with one hand, while his other traced my body. My underwear—which was green and blue like my robes—dissolved at his touch. Literally. It was definitely a cool trick to have in these situations. Suddenly, I was completely bare before him.

"Why do you have so much robe on?" I complained, wiggling under him.

He groaned. "Please stop doing that. I've imagined stripping you naked for a long time—I'd like to enjoy the moment. If you don't stop moving, it's going to be over too quickly."

Ignoring him, I reached up and tugged at his white robes, needing them gone.

He was a control freak, so I expected him to stop me so that he could remove them himself, but he didn't. He let me go, allowing me to be the one to slide them across his body and kick them off the bed.

He wore nothing underneath and I blinked a few times, my mouth back to being drier than the outer areas of Minatsol. Cyrus exuded so much power even against the other gods, so I had no idea why I was surprised to see how big and muscled his body was. His pale skin draped over long lines of heavy muscle. His body just went on and on. *How freaking tall was he?*

"I like the way you stare," he said, watching me while I watched him.

My hands lifted before I could stop them, planting against his firm chest. His skin felt soft and hard at the same time, my fingertips sliding across the smooth surface, tracing the valleys and peaks of his muscles. "You're ... not what I expected," I finally said, not sure if there were better words I could have used. It felt next to impossible to put my true emotions into anything quantitative right then.

"For all of my power," Cyrus said after a click, "I never saw you coming. Even if I had, there is no way I could have prepared myself for you."

His lips slammed closed and I wondered if he regretted that honest statement. I, personally, was very happy to see a softer emotion in him. Even if it had been confusing at the same time. Our moment for exploration came to a close as the need for each other took over. I arched up against Cyrus's hardness and he lowered his chest back down so that his weight was pressed into me.

"Do we need to worry about birth control?" I asked, my mind briefly touching on our previous conversation about the god-children. There was no way I'd let Staviti take my child from me, so I needed to know for certain that it wasn't a possibility.

Cyrus lowered his lips to mine, and just before we touched he said, "You don't have to worry, I will ensure there are no children between us."

Before I could ask another question, his hand slid across my thigh, and he shifted his weight so that he could reach my centre. My breath was shallow as he slid one finger inside of me, followed by another. My body adjusted immediately, and as soon as those low tingles started, I had to move. Every stroke of his fingers had my body winding tighter and tighter. My head fell back and I didn't even care about the little moans leaving my lips, I was too far gone to be embarrassed.

When Cyrus's thumb rubbed across me, I couldn't hold on to my pleasure any longer. It spiralled away from me with enough force that I was light-headed when I finally came back to myself. Deep breaths in and out were pretty much the only function I could manage for a click or two after. Cyrus removed his hand, and I mourned the loss. But I knew we weren't done yet, so it was a short mourning.

Reaching out, I attempted to touch him as well, but he shifted just out of my reach. "I don't need any warming up," he said gruffly.

I had to smile at that. "I didn't need any either," I

chuckled. All of the looking and touching from before had gotten me there no problem. "But I'm not going to complain."

Cyrus's sudden smile was breath-taking. When he reached out and cupped my face, I lifted myself to meet him half way. The moment our lips touched, he slid inside of me, and despite my orgasm not two clicks ago, my body still needed a moment to adjust to fit his size. He held himself inside until I began to move beneath him, unable to bear keeping still any longer. The building heat that had washed away any sense of discomfort was driving me to wrap my legs around his hips and urge him deeper.

He made a low, guttural sound, lifting his head until he could see me properly. There was a strange look on his face—something torn between chastisement and desire. Feeling a tingle of amusement somewhere in the back of my mind, I tightened my hold of him even further, until he gave in with a rumble. He drove into me, his lips crashing back to mine. His pace wasn't slow and careful—it was full of emotion, backed by all of the pent-up frustration that we always had for each other, and I loved it. My hands roamed his muscles—wherever I could reach, drawing sounds and groans from him as his lips moved to my neck, his teeth scraping against my skin. Something shifted, then, and I wasn't sure what it was. I had the oddest sensation of the world tilting around me, of society falling away until only my soul remained, burning brightly with Cyrus's light. I felt as though I was on the edge of a precipice; a choice. I could give in, jump off, submit. I could give him exactly what he had been demanding for so long ... all I had to do was agree.

"Yes," I murmured, just as the tightening in my stomach started again, the pleasure making my head light.

He reached between our bodies, pressing his fingers to my centre and driving me quickly over the edge as the world settled back into place around me with a heavy crash. He held me as I shuddered in his arms, feeling as though I was falling apart at the seams. I felt changed. Altered beyond reasoning. When the final waves passed through my body, he pulled out and switched our positions so fast that I barely had time to steady myself on my knees at the edge of the bed as he slipped off to stand before me. His length was suddenly pressing against my lips, his eyes asking permission, and on instinct I opened my mouth, my tongue moving to cover my teeth. He had barely pressed inside when he exploded, his fingers tight on the back of my neck, his eyes burning in white fire as he watched me.

We collapsed back to the bed afterwards, both of us struggling for breath. I wanted to start panicking, to run off to do damage control on what could potentially have just been a very big mistake ... but instead, I turned on my side, needing to feel connected to the man beside me. It was suddenly necessary for me to be close to him. His eyes found mine, and immediately, the room stopped spinning. It re-centred around him, and my mind quietened. I couldn't sense any turmoil from him, and he didn't look like he was freaking out. His hand was gently stroking my hip, his expression lazily possessive. He was happy that he had claimed me, I realised. At the realisation, I almost snorted.

"Something funny, bug?" His voice was a husky murmur, his eyes warm, despite the nickname.

"You're pleased with yourself," I accused, and I realised that I sounded just the same as him: deeply satisfied, lazy, warm.

What the fuck?

"I told you I would ensure that there were no children between us," he rumbled, his hand gripping my hip tighter, dragging me fully against his body again.

I had to swallow a laugh. "That's ... not what I was talking about." Even though I had not minded it at all.

"What were you talking about then?" He was nuzzling into my neck, his fingers trailing from my hip, to my waist, and back.

I completely lost my train of thought, and somehow ended up pressed beneath him again, his lips still dragging over the tender skin of my neck. One of my legs was bent, half-curled around his waist, cradling the recently-awakened hardness that was pressing insistently against my belly. When he slid inside me again, it was slower than the first time. He rocked me gently to another orgasm, finishing with his lips fused to mine, holding my legs firmly around his waist as he held himself inside me.

Never enough. The thought echoed inside my head, but it held a different taste to my usual thoughts. It sounded like Cyrus. He must have said it out loud, I realised.

"Fuck ... bug," he groaned, rolling off me and tucking me into his side as I tried to recover from the aftershock of tremors that had seized up my body.

I was beginning to like that nickname.

"We can't do this all night," I panted, trying to get my breath back.

"I can't get enough of you," he countered, biting into my shoulder.

I arched back into the touch, my whole body over-sensitised, a heavy breath falling out from between my lips. "I know. You just told me."

He stilled, suddenly turning me around, his eyes locking onto mine. "What?"

"You told me?" I repeated, hesitantly this time. "When we were ... um ... just before. You said 'never enough.'"

Bonded. The word was spoken in his voice, but this time I had a clear view of his mouth ... and it hadn't moved.

"Bonded?" I repeated, my voice shaking.

He was silent and still, only the fractional widening of his eyes cluing me in to the fact that he had heard me.

"Yes ..." he finally croaked out, emotion riding his tone. I had never seen him so open and unguarded before. "We're fucking bonded. You were always meant to be mine."

His mouth crashed back down to mine, then, and I quickly lost myself to the demanding press of his hands. When I felt the hard press of him pushing between my thighs again, I opened my legs to welcome him inside, but a protesting wave of discomfort travelled through my body. We had done this too many times already.

He must have felt it, because he pulled back, a smirk on his face. "Maybe we should give you a break..."

"We should check on Willa," I quickly agreed, my face flushing with heat. If we didn't leave this room, it wouldn't matter how much pain I was in. I couldn't resist him.

"Willa is being guarded by five of the most powerful and *beloved* gods in Topia. She doesn't need you right now, but I sure as fuck do."

This time, the laugh did escape me. "We had sex twice and you're already getting jealous?" I deliberately left out the *bonding* part. I wasn't ready to deal with that just yet.

"How many times do we need to have sex before that's a reasonable emotion?" he asked. "I'll catch up right now."

I laughed again, and the emotion that flooded through me was so alien that it caused me to pause, the laughter dying from my lips. *When had happiness become so foreign to me?*

Not sure I was ready to go there, I focused on another important fact that we'd neglected in our haste to tear each other's robes off.

"We need to warn her about the glitching servers that came after us this sun-cycle," I insisted. "That seems like something they should be aware of."

Cyrus grunted. "Fine. I'll take you to see Willa again, but I will require something in return."

My body heated at the words. Somehow, I already knew what he was asking for. My voice croaked when I finally spoke again. "What is it?"

"You sleep with me from now on."

"Okay." I answered without thinking, the word pulled from me faster than I would have thought possible. I frowned, trying to back-track. "For how long?"

"Until you no longer need me," he answered, without hesitation. "I meant what I said earlier, Emmanuelle. If you want my protection, you will give me everything."

Something about that answer made my heart ache. I didn't like being told what to do, or being blackmailed, but the idea of this arrangement ending at some point made me feel physically ill. Was it even possible for me to separate myself from him now that we had formed some kind of soul-bond? Willa had explained what little she knew of the soul-bond that she had with the Abcurse brothers. Apparently, it was rare enough that it was thought to be gifted by the magic of Topia, not even breakable by the likes of Staviti. But Cyrus thought that we could end this arrangement? My stomach roiled again. The response was so sudden and violent that I had to take a moment to close my eyes and gather myself before I could look at him again.

"Alright," I answered, my voice low. "You have a deal." I pulled myself from the bed then, deciding that if I didn't get up, we'd never leave.

Cyrus was up in an instant as well, and he caught my hand, leading me toward a huge wardrobe. As we stepped inside the room, the lights flickered on, and I gasped. I'd expected the rows of white robes and shoes. The white shirts and belts. Basically, Cyrus had an entire store of white going on. But there was a flash of colour in the back that had shocked me.

My colour.

"It appeared when you first awoke as a god," Cyrus said quietly. "At first I couldn't figure out why they appeared here, in my room. But I think I understand now."

The soul-bond.

His eyes met mine, glowing intensely again, and I realised that he had heard my thought.

Swallowing hard, I quickly looked away from him and stepped closer, my hands brushing across the silken robes as I walked. Blue-green shone brightly in the white palette. There were countless robes, shirts and shorts, and underwear neatly folded in the drawers.

"Unbelievable," I murmured, before shaking my head and reaching for the robes.

No time to ponder the symbolism of what I was seeing—Topia putting my clothes with Cyrus's—it was time to deal with the mess of this world. Before it was too late.

TEN

CYRUS

The way she moved was fucking incredible. Graceful. Nothing like her sister, who had just fallen off the bed and was currently being helped back up by Aros. Willa was unique in her energy, the chaotic nature of it like no other. But Emmy ... she held me captivated.

My head shot around when someone addressed me, and I realised that I'd been completely focused on my female and hadn't heard a word.

"What?" I snapped at Coen, who was standing right in front of me.

He shot me an amused stare, not at all intimidated by the pissed off vibe I was currently rocking. He should have been at least a little cautious. I mean, I was here right now and not inside of Emmy, so I wasn't exactly in the best mood.

"I said, what are we going to do about the servers? Can we figure out if this is a direct attack from Staviti ... or maybe there's something deeper going on?"

"Deeper like...?" I pressed, wondering if he was thinking the same thing as me.

"Like Topia has finally had enough of the bastards destroying this world, and the ancient energy here is fighting back," Siret drawled from where he was sprawled across the end of the bed.

An unfamiliar, and not at all welcomed emotion started to make itself known deep in my chest. My eyes went to Emmy again, and I almost lost focus when I realised that she was looking at me. Not just looking, but devouring me with her gaze. There was so much heat there that for a moment, I completely forgot what we were talking about again.

She was going to be the death of me.

Mine. The thought rang clearly in my head, and I quickly glanced away before I could read her reaction to it. I knew that she would have heard it, but I didn't want to scare her off with the knowledge that we were now unequivocally tied—bound by a power that was beyond us. Bound by the simple flick of fate that we were each other's perfect equal, and we had found each other. There might have been an even chance of me finding another that could have been my perfect equal, but I found *her*. And now it would be only her. For both of our eternities.

That thought didn't scare me as much as it should have, but I knew better than to think it wouldn't frighten her.

"If Topia is the one corrupting those animated with their ancient energy, then we really should check the panteras," I murmured, almost as an afterthought as I realised that Coen was still waiting for a response.

And if we went to the panteras, and found that they were acting out of character, then everyone should be afraid. Because I was created from the deep magic of Topia. The oldest of energies, and if they lost control of me … if I lost control of myself …

All hell would break loose.

Emmy was off the bed and at my side in an instant. "I want to see them," she said, without preamble. "I've been dreaming about meeting them ever since Willa first told me of them."

"I'm going as well," Willa declared, jumping up to stand beside her sister. "I'm sick of being trapped in here. I'll go crazy. I'll do it. Don't think I won't!"

No one doubted that; Willa was halfway there already. When she pressed closer to Emmy, I realised that the two of them actually looked like blood relatives. Willa was a little more petite, her features somehow cute and beautiful at the same time. Emmy was beautiful and refined, the arch of her eyebrows defined, the cut of her cheekbones sharp.

Stunning.

I was too fucking distracted to be dealing with end-of-the-worlds dramas.

"If we're going to do this, we should leave straight away," I said, resigned. I needed to know more than anyone. "And if you two insist on coming as well, despite the fact that this might be a dangerous mission, then I insist that at least three of Abil's sons get their asses there as well, because I'm not taking responsibility for Willa."

Rome scoffed, lifting himself up from where he was propped against a wall. "Firstly, Willa can take care of herself. Don't underestimate her. Secondly, of course we'll be there. Why the hell would you think we wouldn't be?"

"Good morning!" A cheery, sickly sweet voice intoned from the doorway. "Look at my place, filled with so many lovely gods." Pica dragged the word lovely out, because she loved it so much.

"Because of that," I muttered. "Someone has to distract the crazy bitch."

The five of Abil's sons exchanged a glance, and I could see that they were trying to figure out the best way to handle this situation. I enjoyed watching those blessed bastards sweat a little, so I just reached out and pulled Emmy into my side, stepping us away from Willa and her guys.

"What are you doing?" she whispered, pressing her curves into me. I fought back the urge to just disappear us back to my house.

"Watching the show," I returned, giving her a wink.

She tilted her lips in a slow smile, and I almost kissed her. Right there. The only thing that stopped me was the fact that if I kissed her, I would then need to find the closest soft surface.

"What's happening in here, Willy, my little love boo," Pica chirped, dancing closer. She appeared to be dusting the walls, even though she had a block of soap in her hand. It scraped across the furniture as she glided it over the edges. "You're not planning on leaving me, are you? Because that would be very dangerous."

She didn't expand on the danger, and it wasn't

clear if she was referring to danger from her or Staviti.

"Well," Willa started, moving a little closer. "I was hoping to stretch my legs. Just a short walk. I'll be back before you notice me gone."

The soap in Pica's hand exploded; I quickly swung Emmy behind me so that she wasn't pelted with the shards. Rome did the same with Willa, taking the full brunt.

"Whoops," Pica trilled. "Must have squeezed it too tight."

Everyone was on alert then, Abil's sons manoeuvring themselves into defensive positions, fanning out around their girl. Pica wasn't acting in a threatening manner at all, but we all knew she would give no warning if she was about to attack. Her randomness was a skill she'd developed: it gave her an edge in battle.

Pica stepped forward, turning her head to examine her 'Willy boo', and then she nodded. "Yes, some fresh air is exactly what you need. You're looking pale."

Willa didn't argue, she just pushed her way past her bodyguards and smiled brightly. "You're so right Pica. I *love* how right you are."

Pica's return smile was broad and genuine. "Yes, love. Always love."

Then she was gone, back to whatever crazy world she inhabited in her head.

The tension drained from the room and I allowed Emmy to return closer to Willa, now that Willa was no longer a target.

"Let's go, before Pica changes her mind," Yael said in a low voice. "And I for one vote that we don't return, because this place is driving me crazy."

He wasn't actively using his Persuasion, but there were tendrils of it in those words. He was desperate to get away from the love dungeon that Pica had created here for them. Willa quickly hurried about, pulling on some shoes and tying her hair back. Emmy and I waited near the door.

When we made it outside, we walked in the direction of the spot where Pica had chosen to build Willa's house, passing through an elaborate garden. It really did look as though we were all setting out for a walk ... except that I grabbed onto Emmy and Coen grabbed onto Willa as soon as we were out of sight, and the eight of us stepped immediately through a pocket, leaving the platform altogether.

We hadn't discussed where to meet, but we all

ended up in the same place anyway. It was where the panteras usually gathered—almost like a central meeting place for them. It was a short distance from the cave that housed the Mortal Glass, so the reason for their chosen gathering place wasn't such a surprise, if you thought about it. They were the guardians of many things in Topia, and the glass was one of them.

A wave of cold hit me as I glanced around at the clearing, blinking to try and clear the spots of white from my vision.

"Oh my gods," Emmy whispered, her voice small beside me. "It's snowing!"

She sounded equal-parts horrified and excited, and I watched as she ran to the huge, twisted tree by the bank of the river running through the clearing. The Abcurses were also watching as Willa squealed something and did the exact same thing. The girls huddled beneath the cover of the tree together, clutching at each other, looking out at the falling snowflakes.

"It's snowing." That had come from Aros, his tone astounded.

I wasn't sure if this was a good sign or a bad sign, but I knew one thing for certain: it had never snowed in Topia before.

"You don't have to hide," I yelled out to Emmy

and Willa. "This isn't like the acid-snow in Minatsol, it won't cause you any harm."

They ventured out cautiously, and it was then that I realised we were completely alone.

"Where are the panteras?" Rome asked.

"Maybe they're taking refuge from the snow," Emmy supplied. "Is there shelter anywhere near here?"

"The cave," Willa muttered, already turning and marching off.

I caught Aros and Siret passing an amused glance before following after her. "Wrong direction, Rocks," Siret said gently, his hands landing on her shoulders when he caught up to her, turning her the right way.

She didn't even bat an eyelid—just continued in the same determined march, though facing the right direction this time. I slowed behind their group, preferring to walk with Emmy. She seemed nervous, so I wrapped my hand around hers, twisting our fingers together and giving her hand a squeeze. She looked up at me, apparently surprised by the gesture.

"I don't want you running away," I grunted.

"Oh ..." Two fine little wrinkles appeared between her brows as she frowned. "I don't really know how to do the disappearing-and-reappearing thing that you guys do, so …"

"Travelling through pockets," I supplied. "I'll teach you." *Just as soon as I'm sure you won't use it to run away from me.*

"Thank you." Her voice was low, soft, genuine. My hand twitched, and I fought the urge to drag her home and exploit the sudden pliability I could sense from her. It was infuriatingly appealing that all I needed to do to win her over was offer her information.

By the time we reached the cave, the snowing had intensified. Our clothes and hair were dusted in frost, and Siret had been forced to stop and materialise cloaks for everyone. I also had the ability to makes things appear and disappear, but I liked to keep that to myself.

Sure enough, the panteras were gathered below the overhang of the cave opening, several glowing eyes blinking at us from further within. We all stopped before entering, because it wasn't wise to intrude on the creatures uninvited. If any other god had turned up unannounced, they would have already been driven from the land by now, of that much I was certain. Luckily, one of the panteras broke free of the others, moving towards Willa.

"Leden," she greeted, stepping away from the Abcurses and tossing her arms around the pantera's neck.

Leden nudged her affectionately, and we all watched as the two of them seemed to carry out a brief and private conversation, before Leden turned around and disappeared back into the cave. Willa followed, speaking over her shoulder.

"We can go in and light a fire. Leden has asked why we came—I told her that strange things have been happening with the servers."

Strange things have been happening among us, too. The pantera's voice filled my head, apparently projected to each of us, judging by the nervous jolt that ran through Emmy's body. I waited for Leden to elaborate, but she only continued to lead us further into the cave.

"Here will do," Coen finally grumbled. "Willa, do you want to light a fire?"

"It might burn us all down," she replied dryly.

I heard another of the Abcurses chuckle, but it was now too dark to see which one it had been.

"Just concentrate," Aros soothed her. "You won't hurt anyone. Start small."

There was silence, then, and I set my hands against Emmy's hips as I waited, drawing her back into me. The cloak was an unwanted barrier between us, but I didn't want her to get cold, so I allowed it to remain. When she rested her head back against my chest, I tried to tell myself that she didn't already own every piece of me.

After half a click, a small ball of flame burst to life, illuminating Willa's face, set in deep concentration. She crouched, setting the little fire against the ground before running her hands through the flames, encouraging them to grow. It was fascinating to watch, but as soon as there was enough light to see by, I wasted no time in redirecting my attention to Emmy. She wasn't frightened at all. There was an almost feverish look in her eye, a hunger for answers that made me grin.

The panteras didn't stand a chance.

ELEVEN

EMMY

Panteras were like nothing I'd ever experienced before. I could almost feel the wealth of knowledge contained amongst them. It wouldn't surprise me at all if they knew everything. Literally every single thing there was to know about both worlds.

I need it ... I needed the information.

Cyrus's hand tightened minutely on my forearm, and I tilted my head back to see him. He wore a lazy grin, looking far more relaxed than I'd seen in a long time.

"Which one are you going to start with?" he asked me.

I didn't bother to play dumb, I never liked that game. "That one," I said, inclining my head just enough so that he knew which pantera I referred to. I didn't know if it was a male or female, but it was beautiful. Like Willa's pantera, only its coat was black. Black as the darkest night sky. It was shiny as well, like velvet draped across a powerful body.

One kick could kill me, that much was clear. Or … the old me anyway. Gods were a little harder to knock off.

"Sparrow," Cyrus murmured, almost sounding pleased. "He's an elder. One of the oldest pantera that I know of."

Knowledge. That was basically what he was saying. Old equalled experience.

"That's the one," I decided.

And I guess that I don't get a say in this decision?

The voice filtered through my head, and for a beat I was too frozen to register what had happened. It was only because I'd heard a pantera just before, when we first arrived, that I knew who was speaking.

Apologies, I started, unsure if I'd been unnecessarily rude or not. *I didn't realise you could hear our conversation. I would very much like to speak with you.*

There was a brush of something across my body, sending trills down it. It felt like power, like the sort of power Cyrus wielded, only a hundred times stronger.

You crave knowledge, Sparrow stated. *Beware of learning more than your mind can handle.*

Willa had said they were cryptic, something that frustrated her to no end. Me, on the other hand? I absolutely loved riddles. I found myself stepping closer. Cyrus remained at my side and it felt nice to have him there. Most of my life I'd had Willa, but she always needed a lot of help with ... everything. She was strong in her own way. Strength of character being the top of that list, but she was often in trouble that I had to save her from. I had to be the mature, capable part of our duo. It felt, in this circumstance, that I could rely on Cyrus to help me. I could relinquish some of my control.

As I moved closer, the panteras shifted away from Sparrow, leaving a space around him for me to step into. Cyrus remained a little behind. Close enough to help if needed, but not crowding me.

Hello, Fertility, Sparrow greeted me politely.

"You can tell?" I blurted out loud. The mind-talking thing was a little too weird for me.

If a pantera's snout could grin, I felt like this pantera might be doing just that.

I can tell. But you are not here to talk to me about your gift. You seek other knowledge.

The tone of his voice was so deep and rich, it sent trills down my spine every time he spoke in my head.

"The servers," I started, "there's something wrong with them. They're violent. Uncontrollable. I'm worried about what this might mean."

Sparrow lifted his head and I turned to find him locking eyes with Cyrus. I wondered if they were talking to each other.

Cyrus gave a single nod of his head. "I feel no loss of control," he finally said out loud. "My power is as it always was."

What were they talking about? I took a step closer to Cyrus, and his entire attention fixed on me.

"Your power?" I asked.

The colour of his eyes deepened. "I am born of the energy of Topia. If others born of the same energy are starting to be affected, then it stands to reason that …"

"You might start wielding axes and making groaning noises too," I finished for him, dread sinking into me as I swung to Sparrow. "Is that possible? Can Cyrus be corrupted like the others?"

Huge dark eyes regarded me. *Anything is possible.*

In regards to the Neutral energy, it will all depend on the strength of the vessel. On the strength of the heart. Cyrus is much more than just his energy. Have faith, young friend.

"You should have said something," a hard voice cut in from the side.

I'd temporarily forgotten that Willa and her guys were there, and I was a little surprised to see Yael and Siret standing close by.

Yael was the one who'd spoken, and he took a step even closer. "If you lose control of your power, Neutral, all of us will be fucked. That isn't something you should be waiting to tell us."

Cyrus crossed his arms, arching a single eyebrow in Yael's direction. "Something you should have figured out for yourselves, isn't it? Everyone knows I am born of the Topian energy."

Yael threw his hands in the air, massive bicep muscles framing either side of his head. "There's more than one thing going on right now. And to be honest, I don't think about you much Cyrus, so your power isn't on my mind a lot. Just tell us next time."

Cyrus's power bristled across his skin. He didn't like being reprimanded, but when Yael's head swung toward Willa, who was standing next to her impressive fire, I felt Cyrus calm down.

He understood why the Abcurses were so upset. Anything that put Willa in danger was a sore point with them.

"I will be upfront in the future," Cyrus conceded. "I was mainly waiting to see if the pantera had been effected, but so far they are as normal."

Energy washed over the entire cave then and I found myself plastered back against Cyrus, his arm banding protectively around me. Yael and Siret were in my line of vision and I noticed that while they also looked worried, there was amusement in their gazes as they watched Cyrus and me.

Pantera are affected. A chorus of voices echoed in my head. It sounded like the entire herd were speaking to us. *We have lost five of our members.*

There was a heavy moment. A mourning feel to the air.

They disappeared, unable to remain with us. They said they felt ... different. That they were being called away. We haven't seen them since.

Willa rushed toward Leden—the pantera she had bonded with—her face creased in sadness. "What can we do?" she cried, burying her head in Leden's neck.

The Abcurses closed in behind her, looking

casual as anything, but it was clear that they were on high alert.

Leden's answer was lost to anyone but Willa, as they began to communicate in silence—the small sounds that Willa released were the only indication that they were even having a conversation. Eventually, she turned, and her eyes flicked between the Abcurses before finding me.

"We have to prepare for a fight," she finally announced. "It's clear that something has happened to upset the balance of the worlds, and I'm pretty sure that whatever it was ... it has something to do with us. Maybe it's my power, maybe it's the fact that I somehow brought Emmy back to life, or maybe it's that I returned from the imprisonment realm and dragged my mother with me—"

"I'm sensing a theme here," Cyrus noted dryly. "When you said it has something to do with *us,* you meant it was *your* fault, right?"

I glanced back over my shoulder at him and his eyes met mine briefly before he looked back to Willa, his hand tightening in its grip on my waist. He was pretending not to see the warning in my eyes.

"Whatever's happening is *not* your fault," I spoke up, before one of the Abcurses could jump in to defend her.

I shoved Cyrus's arm away in my censure, taking a step forward. He also took a step forward, his hands finding my shoulders and dragging me back to rest against his front again. He was warm and strong, a solid force to ward off the creepy vibes I was getting from the cave, so I didn't try to break away again. I wasn't sure that I really had the strength to stay away from Cyrus, and I didn't think that I wanted to, deep down.

"I should go and see them ..." Willa muttered, almost to herself.

I was confused, and Cyrus was clearly confused —judging by the fact that he didn't immediately voice an opinion. The Abcurses, however, picked up on her meaning immediately, possibly hearing an errant thought in her head.

"Hell no," Rome grunted, as the others shook their heads.

"They could be hostile." Siret seemed to agree with his brother, his brow furrowing. "That's why they left the rest of the herd and exiled themselves."

"Willa," I said sternly, forcing her eyes back to mine. "This is *not* your fault, and you don't have to put yourself in danger to fix it."

"It might give us an advantage over Staviti, if there's going to be a battle," she explained, appealing to all of us. Beside her, Leden made a *humming* sound of approval. "I doubt that he even cares about the servers malfunctioning. He probably sent them straight to the banishment cave. If we can figure out what's happening to the magic of Topia, we can use that knowledge against him."

I could feel my brows shooting up in surprise, but I tried to quickly wipe the emotion from my face. Everyone was quiet for a click, mulling over what she had said, but then Aros finally spoke.

"She's right—we do need to figure out what's going wrong with the magic of Topia, and it will arm us well in a battle against Staviti. But if we don't get her back to Pica within the next rotation, that woman is going to take the crazy up a notch and we need her on our side—and reasonably stable. She's our best weapon right now."

"We'll go," I quickly offered, before I could think too hard about it.

"We will?" Cyrus's question rumbled through me, since he had pulled me so tightly against his body.

I felt my lips twitching at the undertone of amusement in his question. Coen snorted out a laugh.

"Fine." I shrugged casually. "I'll go myself."

"No, *we* will go," he snapped out. "We had a deal, bug. Your safety is now my concern."

"What's the deal?" Willa asked casually, ever-considerate of sensitive topics and situations.

"I think it's a private deal," Coen muttered quietly, his tone laced with humour.

"What private deal?" she asked, even louder.

The panteras around us started to shift about—some in amusement, some in annoyance. They were on edge, clearly. Willa's sudden tonal shift probably wasn't helping things. She seemed to realise the same thing, because she lowered her voice to a loud whisper.

"Are you making private deals with my sister?" she accused Cyrus. "Without making an honest woman out of her and offering for her hand?"

I knew that she was joking, but Cyrus didn't seem to. His arm dropped, his hands landing on my shoulders again and spinning me around, his head ducking down a little to fix me with a puzzled expression.

"You're not an honest woman?" he asked.

I tried to hold in my amusement, but a male laugh behind me had Cyrus's confusion deepening.

"It's a dweller custom," Willa explained patiently. *Wow, she was convincing.* "A dweller woman can't lay with a man out of wedlock. If she does, she becomes a dishonest woman."

Cyrus frowned at me. "When does this dishonesty start?"

Willa let out a shout of triumph as I rolled my eyes.

"I *knew* you two had slept together!" she shouted, causing the panteras to stir again.

Cyrus was switching his attention from her to me, his alarm growing. "We need to get wedlocked," he said firmly. "Who here can wedlock us?"

"Anyone can do it." Willa shrugged casually, moving into my line of sight. "You just need a few rings and you need to repeat some words and make a few promises."

"What kind of promises?" Cyrus asked, as I started to wonder if the joke had maybe gone a little too far. "I haven't brushed up on dweller customs in a long time."

"That you will belong to each other completely and forever," Willa explained, a smile of mischief beginning to light up her face. "That you will love and protect each other."

Cyrus waved his hand dismissively. "We have already made such promises."

I blanched as Willa turned an astonished stare on me.

"No we haven't!" I squeaked.

"Yes we have," Cyrus countered. "Have you forgotten? I can take you back to my home and remind you."

Willa started laughing, until she realised that the Abcurses had all gathered around her, frowns on their faces.

"What?" she asked them, spinning around. "Oh *hell* no. It was a *joke,* guys!"

"Why didn't you tell us about the dweller wedlocking rule?" Yael asked, his green eyes narrowed almost dangerously. "Willa-toy, you belong to us. We should be wedlocked in the dweller way."

"We are *not* having this conversation right now!" She tossed her hands up in the air, walked to my side and grabbed my arm before marching me toward the opening of the cave.

"Well that backfired," I noted casually.

"Shut up," she tossed back. "I can't believe you didn't tell me you slept with Neutral."

"Will! It only *just* happened." I groaned, lowering my voice as the others approached behind us. "Are you really upset?"

"No, not really," she sulked, kicking her foot against the ground. "I just don't want him to steal you away from me."

"He won't," I promised.

"He might," Cyrus countered, stepping up beside me.

He sounded serious. Willa scowled at him, but I focused my gaze ahead, trying to ignore the sudden pounding of my heart inside my chest.

TWELVE

CYRUS

Two rotations later, we were gathered once again in Willa's cleverly-designed jail cell, or 'bedroom' as Pica insisted on calling it. Willa was sitting on the very end of the bed, Rome and Yael either side of her, the others stationing themselves around the room at seemingly deliberate vantage-points. Each of them had a clear view of both Willa and the door.

Not that I blamed them.

Emmy was securely tucked under my arm, and I was on high-alert. She had initially tried to wiggle away from me, growing skittish from the looks that Willa kept throwing at her. Each time she tried to escape, I released her shoulder and rested my hand against the back of her neck. It calmed her every single time, like magic. I had no idea *why*, just as I had no idea why I loved the fact so much, but I wasn't going to look a gift-pantera in the mouth.

So my girl liked when I touched her neck? I wasn't going to start complaining, just as long as she didn't allow anyone else to touch her this way. After the first few escape attempts, she gave up. Now she was cuddled up into my side, her hands tucked up against her body as her head rested lightly against my chest.

I had a feeling she was exhausted, and I hardly blamed her. The last few sun-cycles that we had endured were enough to exhaust even me. And she had died and returned as a god in that time. I wanted to drag her home and put her to bed, but we had to discuss our situation first.

"I have received word from the others," Pica announced, breezing her way back into the room, her robes fanning out and fluttering about with the briskness of her movements.

She frowned at Yael and Rome—who left no room for her to sit beside Willa—before she pulled up a chair and sat down with a flourish, crossing her legs and fussing with her robe.

"Will they come?" Coen asked from his position

up against a dresser, his shoulders resting back against the wall.

"Of course!" Pica responded the same way as she had the first time we had asked that question, a rotation ago. We had thought that she was just being overtly-optimistic then, so we were all a little surprised to hear the same answer again.

"Really?" Siret quirked a brow. "Everyone you sent messages to agreed to stand with us in a war against Staviti?"

Pica fluttered her fingers, trying to brush away his statement. "They agreed to come to a party. We'll ask them at the party."

Willa groaned, and I heard the short puff of frustration that escaped Emmy, though she managed to keep her cool.

"When is the party?" I asked, mulling over the idea.

It wasn't a bad one, as far as Pica's ideas went. If we asked the gods in person, I would be able to see their faces when they answered. I would know if they were lying or not. Knowing our enemies was almost more important than knowing our friends.

"Seven sun-cycles from now," Pica answered jovially. "Not enough time for preparations, to be sure!"

"Why is she happy about that?" Emmy muttered, only loud enough for me to hear.

I slipped my hand up along the line of her delicate shoulders, my fingers pushing beneath her hair and spanning out over the back of her neck. She relaxed instantly, the tension draining out of her.

Fuck. I loved that.

"What is there to prepare?" Willa asked.

Pica clapped her hands together, apparently delighted at being asked to explain something. "We must find and secure a location," she explained. "And then we will need to ward it against attacks. While our guests might not all know the reason for this gathering, Staviti will certainly know. We might end up trapped there—so we must prepare appropriate provisions, shelters, and escape routes if possible. Oh, and the most important thing of all! We must prepare *you!*"

"Me?" Willa released the word on a strangled sound, apparently still trying to wrap her head around the gravity of everything Pica had just told her in the happiest and most excited of voices.

"If the gods are to turn on Staviti, they need to know that Staviti's equal is also standing with them, or else they will be too afraid."

"I'm not Staviti's equal," she blurted.

The Abcurses looked like they were about to jump in and insist that she was, so I quickly spoke. "You might not be, but they don't need to know that. The more powerful you look and seem, the more likely it will be that they will stand with you. If you show weakness or accidentally set yourself on fire ... you might as well say goodnight to this little rebellion, because it won't ever see the light of day."

"Great pep talk," Willa muttered dryly, her eyes rolling up to the ceiling, before she seemed to gather herself, turning her attention back to Pica. "I'll do whatever you think I need to. I'll be ready."

"Good," I said quickly, before Pica could do any number of the things that she was likely about to do, like squeal or start clapping her hands again. "Then we can start preparations in the next sun-cycle, and we should also prepare Emmanuelle because ..." I trailed off, a surge of protectiveness falling over me.

My words died, my fingers tightening their hold on the back of Emmy's neck. She startled, glancing up at me, but I avoided her eyes. I couldn't allow Pica to know what Emmy really was. I couldn't let *any* of the gods know what Emmy really was. It didn't matter that she would prove to be Willa's greatest asset in winning people over to our side. The only thing that mattered was that Staviti would want her dead—and she was an easier target than Willa.

Everyone was staring at me, waiting for me to finish. I tried again, but the words still wouldn't come. I simply couldn't put her in that kind of danger.

"Tired," I finally finished. "She's tired. So I should take her back to sleep."

"Fertility," the little traitor quickly pushed the word out before I could yank her through a pocket and give her something better to do with her mouth. "That's my gift ... fertility. Life ..." I could tell that she was looking at Willa, who had tears in her eyes.

Something passed between the two girls, causing the tears in Willa's eyes to spill over, though she didn't actually appear to be upset. I was assuming that this was just another extension of all the crying she did when she woke up and thought that Emmy was dead. Emmy had reminded her.

"I guess that makes sense, in a way," Willa said, swiping at her cheeks. "I wanted to give you life. I wanted you to live. I kept thinking it over and over. If I was going to somehow turn you into a god of anything, it makes sense that it would be the one thing I was thinking when all of this happened. I wanted you to be filled with life again."

"You won't repeat this to anyone," I warned Pica, who had gone eerily silent, her wide eyes fixed on Emmy.

"They will want to know ..." Pica said unsurely, the warmth and happiness sucked from her tone. There was a glimpse of something real beneath—something soaked in pain and loss. It was hardly surprising, since Pica had always wanted her child back. Eternity was a long time to live without your greatest desire.

"This is my decision." I allowed power to leak into my voice and infect the room.

The others all took notice, and Pica finally tore her gaze away from Emmy to meet my eyes. I knew that I was glowing, and Pica knew what that meant. I was exercising my authority over her, warning her away from this line that I would not allow her to cross. Emmy was mine: I had made her a promise, and I *would* protect her. Pica ducked her head down in a silent acknowledgement before turning on her heel and leaving the room. There was silence after that; no one was prepared to break the heavy tension my power left behind, like a coating that couldn't be removed. Emmy was the only one brave enough.

"We won't let Staviti win," she declared, stepping forward. "He's been controlling both worlds for too long. It's time to take the power back. We can do this."

Willa was up and throwing her arms around Emmy before I could blink. "You're right, Em," she said, sounding teary again. "And do you know why we're going to win?" She paused, like she was waiting for someone to answer. When no one did, she continued on. "Because we have something Staviti never will. A true family that will stick together and fight for each other. Until the very end. We will never give up," she declared.

For the first time since Emmy had died, since I faced Staviti on that cliff top, the tight ball of tension in my chest loosened ... because Willa was right. Despite all of the odds, I was now part of a family.

Emmy was mine. Willa was her sister. The Abcurses were bonded to Willa.

This was my damn family.

I was no longer alone, and in that moment, I knew that there was nothing I wouldn't do to keep them all safe.

Staviti had chosen the wrong family to mess with. His sun-cycles were now numbered.

ALSO BY JANE WASHINGTON

Standalone Books

I Am Grey

The Bastan Hollow Saga

Book One: Charming (Dec, 2018)

Book Two: Disobedience (Jan, 2019)

Book Three: Fairest (Feb, 2019)

Book Four: Prick (Mar, 2019)

Book Five: Animal (Apr, 2019)

Curse of the Gods Series

Book One: Trickery

Book Two: Persuasion

Book Three: Seduction

Book Four: Strength

Book Five: Pain (Oct, 2018)

Seraph Black Series

Book One: Charcoal Tears

Book Two: Watercolour Smile

Book Three: Lead Heart

Book Four: A Portrait of Pain

Beatrice Harrow Series

Book One: Hereditary

Book Two: The Soulstoy Inheritance

ALSO BY JAYMIN EVE

Secret Keepers Series

Book One: House of Darken

Book Two: House of Imperial

Book Three: House of Leights

Book Four: House of Royale (September 15th 2018)

Storm Princess Series

Book One: The Princess Must Die (September 1st 2018)

Book Two: The Princess Must Strike (October 1st)

Book Three: The Princess Must Reign (November 1st)

Curse of the Gods Series

Book One: Trickery

Book Two: Persuasion

Book Three: Seduction

Book Four: Strength

Book Five: Pain (October 2018)

NYC Mecca Series

Book One: Queen Heir

Book Two: Queen Alpha

Book Three: Queen Fae

Book Four: Queen Mecca (2017)

A Walker Saga

Book One: First World

Book Two: Spurn

Book Three: Crais

Book Four: Regali

Book Five: Nephilius

Book Six: Dronish

Book Seven: Earth

Supernatural Prison Trilogy

Book One: Dragon Marked

Book Two: Dragon Mystics

Book Three: Dragon Mated

Supernatural Prison Stories

Broken Compass

Magical Compass

Louis (December 2018)

Hive Trilogy

Book One: Ash

Book Two: Anarchy

Book Three: Annihilate

Sinclair Stories

Songbird

CONNECT WITH JANE WASHINGTON

Website:
www.janewashington.com
Email:
inquiries@janewashington.com
Facebook:
@janewashingtonbooks
Instagram:
@janewashingtonbooks
Twitter:
@TheAuthorPerson

CONNECT WITH JAYMIN EVE

Website:
www.jaymineve.com
Email:
jaymineve@gmail.com
Facebook:
@JayminEve.Author
Instagram:
@jaymineve
Twitter:
@jaymineve1

Printed in Great Britain
by Amazon